Shadows
on a White Wall

by Emilee Hines

Emilee Hines

Shadows on a White Wall

by

Emilee Hines

Emilee Hines

Shadows on a White Wall

by

Emilee Hines

Shadows on a White Wall

by

Emilee Hines

Acknowledgments

The Marbury Hill house is based mainly on a stately home named Clarkton, where I often visited in my youth. The plantation is a composite of many estates I visited in writing the Old Virginia Houses series. The characters and events are from my imagination.

My thanks go to my daughter Catherine Cantieri, who designs such beautiful book covers, to my patient husband Gerald Liedl, who helps me with computer problems, and to my cousin Jack Moorefield, who sent me a picture of Clarkton as it looks now.

You may also like these books by Emilee Hines.

Fiction:

Voting for Love

The Christmas Dance

The Proposal

Callie's Choice

A Place to Love

Burnt Station

Nonfiction:

It Happened in Virginia

Til Death Do Us Part

East African Odyssey

All of these books are available from Amazon.com in print and electronic form. Visit Emilee's author page on Amazon, or her website: www.emileehines.com. You can also contact her at:

Emilee Hines

206 Carriage Park Summit

Hendersonville, NC 28791

or

emilee214@att.net

Chapter 1

Even before I went to Marbury Hill, my life was filled with both good things and bad. Sometimes it was hard to tell which was which, but looking back later, I could see where each decision was a turning point.

One of them was the blustery day in early March when I arrived.

As the Amtrak pulled away, I stood alone with my suitcase on the graveled parking lot. The few other passengers who'd gotten off were getting into cars, or walking arm in arm with someone who'd come to meet them.

No one had come for me. Jason Ashby was supposed to; he'd made that clear in the email that accompanied my ticket. I was on the right train, and it was a few minutes late, rather than early, so he should have been here waiting. I shivered and pulled my woolen hat closer over my ears.

In March, weather could be warm with the flush of an early spring, or wintry with the bite of a cold wind. This time it had decided to be wintry. No matter how unprofessional I might look, I was glad I'd worn pants, a coat, gloves and a thick wooly knitted hat. It wasn't as if I had to make a good impression—after all, I had the job, if I wanted it. I took out my cell phone and pulled off one glove to make dialing easier. I scrambled in my purse for the slip of paper I'd written the Ashbys' number on.

"You lost, ma'am?" a deep, obviously southern voice asked. I turned to see a big man in jeans, boots and a plaid fleece jacket. He could have been a model for an L.L. Bean catalog, with the rugged, slightly unkempt look that said Outdoorsman.

"I was expecting someone to meet me," I said. "I'm supposed to go to Marbury Hill."

"I don't know why you'd want to go there, but I can take you."

"I wouldn't want to trouble you," I said, puzzled by his remark. Why wouldn't I want to go there? "Mr. Ashby will probably be here in a few minutes."

"Oh, it's no trouble. I live out next to the plantation. If we meet him on the way, I'll hit the horn and stop him."

"Well, all right," I said, sure that my doubt hung in my voice.

"Your ride won't be as fancy or comfortable as it would if Mr. Ashby came for you, but since he hasn't, you're stuck with me." He picked up my suitcase and strode off. I ran to catch up with him, wishing I'd thought to wear boots as he did. Pulling open the door to an extended cab pickup, he flung my suitcase into the back and held the door for me. *Rugged, but a gentleman*, I thought. And who was he? I was about to ride off into unknown country with a strange man.

"I'm Adam Carrington," he said, as if he'd read my mind. "I'm Marian Ashby's cousin."

"I'm Kate Flynn."

"Irish background," he said. "I'd have known even without the name. The blue eyes and black hair give you away." He climbed into the truck, slammed the door and buckled his seat belt. I did likewise. He started the engine and we bumped across the parking lot and then shot out onto a narrow blacktop road. Snow was beginning to fall, and whoever or whatever he was, I was glad not to be standing outside in the cold.

I tried to make a joke. "'Give me away'? You make it sound as if I'm trying to hide something."

"No, just observing." He paused. "Are you hiding something? Are you Jason's girlfriend?"

"Of course not! Why would you think that?"

"I'm racking my brain to think why else you would be coming to Marbury Hill in the tail end of winter."

"I'm here for a job." Suddenly I felt defensive. Mr. Ashby's descriptions had made Marbury Hill sound lovely, and the job a real plum.

"Doing what? They have a housekeeper."

"Mr. Ashby said I'll be Mrs. Ashby's social secretary."

He gave a short bark of laughter. "Social secretary? Keeper is more like it."

"What do you mean?"

He sighed. "My cousin's … not quite right. Sometimes she's just a little nutty, sometimes wildly off base. But most of the time she has good, rational days and seems very normal. One thing she doesn't need is a social secretary. She doesn't give parties, never has, so she doesn't need to write fancy invitations. She sometimes calls or texts me, but I don't know anyone else she corresponds with."

I was starting to get nervous. Was Adam Carrington testing me, perhaps exaggerating or even lying for some unknown reason? Or had Jason Ashby misled me? And why hadn't he come to meet me?

I tried to study both my surroundings and my driver. He drove easily, one hand on the wheel, the other lying against his thigh. He wore no gloves, and his hands looked tan and strong as he reached to turn on the heater. A welcome flow of warm air came at me from the floor as well as dashboard vents.

He gestured toward the vents. "Okay? Too hot or cold?"

"It's fine," I said. "Is it usually this cold here in March?"

"Can be even colder and we could even have more snow tonight." He gestured toward the snow falling all round us, beginning to whiten the dead grass along the roadside. "Not sticking on the roads yet." Then he abruptly changed the subject. "How long you planning to stay?"

"I don't really know. I'm on a trial basis for a month."

He glanced back at my suitcase. "You travel light."

"I can send for whatever I need. I just don't know yet what that might be."

"True."

He was silent for a mile or so. I studied the few modest houses and mobile homes we passed, and realized that this was a rather low-income area. Would Marbury Hill be as decrepit as some of these dwellings? We soon left even those buildings behind, and headed downhill through a forest of leafless trees, their limbs dark against the gray sky.

We crested a hill, dropping down so rapidly I caught my breath, then crested another hill and fled downward toward a stream. Just before I thought we'd go into the water, he braked sharply and made an oblique turn across a narrow wooden bridge. At the opposite end he turned again and we headed uphill, the engine laboring in a lower gear.

"That bridge is dangerous," I said, my chest tight. "It's set at the wrong angle."

"You're right. The highway department put it in where the creek was the narrowest, and where there were rock outcroppings on both sides to anchor it. Everybody knows you have to slow down for it. Or almost everybody. A few reckless souls have missed the turn and ended up in the creek." He shrugged.

At the top of the hill the road flattened out and we passed several fields, tan with stubble from last year's corn stalks sticking up through the red-brown earth. Farmhouses were set back from the road with long dirt driveways. Then we were in woods again.

"My land starts here," he said.

I saw no obvious marker, but a short distance farther on he indicated a graveled driveway that ran beside a red mailbox. "My humble abode." Not nearly as fine as Marbury Hill, but it suits me."

After a few moments' silence, he asked, "Why didn't you drive here?"

"No car. I could have rented one, but Mr. Ashby said I wouldn't need it, since he and Mrs. Ashby have two and if I rented one it would just sit idly and cost me a bundle."

He turned briefly toward me. "It would only cost a bundle if you stay a long time. Without it, you're trapped."

"Trapped? That seems a little..."

"Harsh? Well, it's a harsh situation: you're going into an unknown area with no escape plan. It's just up here." He turned into a crumbling paved drive bordered by dark cedars. Snow had begun to stick in shady spots, and the road lay white and trackless. We moved backward into another world, tranquil but eerie.

I felt guilty for listening to him talk about the Ashbys, even as I wished he'd said more. If Jason Ashby hadn't been honest about the job, what else hadn't he been honest about? After months of job hunting, I was so grateful for his offer that I hadn't minded coming to a place as isolated as Marbury Hill, and I hadn't asked many questions about just what the job entailed. Something about his manner had put me at ease when I met him to discuss the job last month in a coffee shop near downtown Richmond. I was beginning to realize that I should have asked more questions, but at the same time I was annoyed at this gruff man who didn't seem to like his cousin, her husband—or me.

As we drove on, half a dozen buzzards flew up from something dead in the road and alighted on bare-limbed trees. He pulled over and got out of the car, turning to me before shutting the door. "Don't look," he shook his head. "Poor possum. They're so slow and ugly I feel sorry for them. I stop and move them whenever I see one on the road, but most people run them over. Possums and groundhogs both. They mean no harm, but they die just the same."

Despite his telling me not to look, or maybe because he did, I looked, and shivered at the sight of bare teeth protruding from a bloody carcass. He straddled the dead possum and tossed it to the side of the road. As we drove off I looked behind us to see the buzzards swooped down again on their prey.

The road was scarcely wide enough for Adam Carrington's pickup and he drove with such speed and verve that I had to brace against the dash when he hit potholes. Just when I thought we must surely be lost, our way was barred by tall black iron gates set into a rock wall that stretched off into the woods as far as I could see. A pull chain hung to one side, and as Adam Carrington jerked on it, the gates slowly swung open and we passed through.

I saw Marbury Hill for the first time, white walls against the gray sky, tall chimneys on each side and towering white pillars that spanned two stories to the roof. Dead leaves littered the lawn and banked against the steps. A black network of vines clung to the walls, and all the windows across the front were shrouded. One shutter hung lopsidedly. Marbury Hill looked desolate and neglected.

The only sign of life was smoke curling from both chimneys, so at least someone was home. I realized I'd been holding my breath, my imagination elaborating on Mr. Carrington's warnings. I let out my breath slowly. I was here, ready to face whatever was ahead of me—and I had to admit that I was looking forward to seeing Jason Ashby again.

Adam Carrington swung the pickup around in a spray of gravel before the front portico and put the vehicle in Park. "Last chance to change your mind," he said. "I'll be glad to take you back to town. Or to my place until tomorrow's train."

I shook my head. "Thanks anyway." *Staying at a stranger's house overnight? Talk about entering an unknown area with no escape plan*, I thought. Was that the real reason he was trying to talk me out of staying at Marbury Hill?

"At least take my phone number in case you need help," he said. He repeated it and made sure I keyed it into my phone.

"Well, thanks for the ride and all the information," I said, trying to lighten the mood again. "And don't blame yourself if I get in trouble; you did what you could to dissuade me." I gave him a smile he didn't return.

"Listen, you can get to my place in a few minutes if you go out the side door and keep walking past the gardens and the stable, then head down toward the river. You'll see a bridle path. My house used to be the overseer's residence."

"I'll be all right," I said, with more confidence than I felt. I hated to admit it, but he'd frightened me.

He came around to open the door and set my suitcase on the stone floor of the portico. "Don't lose that train ticket," he said. Then, with a little bow, he got in the pickup and drove off.

I watched him go, torn between feeling that I had lost a potential lifeline and feeling annoyed for how effectively he'd spooked me. Snowflakes drifted down and fell onto bronze oak leaves, obliterating his tracks so that after a few moments I could scarcely see that he'd been there. I shook my head to dispel the unease I was feeling, and realized that I was still standing out in the cold. I mounted the two steps, picked up my suitcase and brought the heavy brass knocker against the door.

Chapter 2

When no one answered, I brought the knocker down again, harder. What if no one let me in? I could call Mr. Carrington, but in the meantime, my feet were growing numb with cold. I thrust my hands into my armpits, hugging myself for warmth.

The door swung open, but it was blocked by a large woman in a dress that came down to her calves, a saggy gray cardigan and a big white apron. "Yes?" she demanded, looking me up and down.

"I'm Kate Flynn, Mr. Ashby is expecting me."

She stepped back and closed the door in my face. I heard her retreating steps, then a voice saying, "Oh, damn! Yes, let her in."

The woman returned, opened the door and without a word reached for my suitcase. "Mr. Ashby's in the library." She led me down a blue carpeted hallway. Ahead and above, a magnificent stairway rose curving to the upper level. She nodded to a paneled door that opened off the hallway. I pushed it open and entered a large room, where a welcoming fire crackled in the fireplace.

Jason Ashby turned from the fireplace, put down his pipe into a brass ashtray and came forward with outstretched hands and a big smile. Over the pungence of the fire I could smell his pipe tobacco, rich and slightly acidic. "Miss Flynn, I am so sorry for leaving you stranded at the station! I got distracted by Marian, and simply lost track of the time. Say, how did you get here? Taxis are almost nonexistent."

He looked much the same as he had in that coffee-shop interview a few weeks ago: unnervingly handsome. He was just shy of six feet tall with an athletic build that reminded me of the guys on my college's soccer team, although he was almost certainly 20 years past college age. His dark brown hair was relatively short, with a slight artful dishevelment that made him look relaxed, and his face had the classical lines of a Renaissance sculpture. But it was his eyes that really stood out: they were the sienna brown of a hawk's eyes, but with gold flecks that twinkled every time he smiled.

Part of me had hoped that his arms were outstretched for a hug, but instead he clasped my right hand with both his hands and shook it warmly. I got the awful feeling that I might be blushing, and made a deliberate effort to tone down the big smile on my face.

"A Mr. Carrington was kind enough to bring me. He said he lived nearby." I decided instinctively not to mention what he'd told me. Jason didn't need to hear that sort of thing right now.

He looked startled. "Well, what a coincidence! Did he say anyone had sent him?"

That's an odd question, I thought, but at least I could answer it honestly: "No, I think he was just in town running some errands."

"Ah," he nodded, satisfied with my answer. "Well, I'm glad you made it. It looks like we might have snow, and I feel terrible just thinking of you standing at that station in the cold. Why didn't you call?"

"I was about to when Mr. Carrington approached and asked if I were lost. I thought there might have been something happening here to delay you."

"And you were right. Can you forgive me?" He smiled, the gold in his eyes sparkling. "Here," he said, taking my hand and leading me to a seat by the fire. "Let me take your coat," Before I could remove the coat myself, he was sliding it off my shoulders, his hands warm against me. He laid my coat across an armchair and went to the door, calling, "Hattie, could you bring us some coffee?"

He came back to stand beside me, the fragrance of him—his pipe tobacco, his aftershave and a woodsy smell from the fireplace—stirred my senses so that I almost had to close my eyes to keep from looking at him. I knew deep down that I hadn't inquired too deeply into what my job duties would be because I had been pulled into his orbit. I needed a job, and he'd made the position at Marbury Hill sound ideal, but part of the attraction of the offer was the man making it.

Stop it! I scolded myself. *His wife may or may not be insane, but you will be if you let yourself get involved with your* married *employer. It's the oldest cliché out there. Get control of your feelings and tomorrow you can leave.*

The woman he called Hattie, the one who'd opened the door to me, came in carrying a silver tray that she set down on a low table by the fireplace. On it was a silver coffee pot, two white china cups and saucers, a tiny cream pitcher, a sugar bowl, linen napkins and a china plate holding slices of fruit cake and several small sandwiches with the crusts cut off. How had she managed all that in such a short time?

"That looks delicious, thank you," I said, and I saw a quick smile cross her face and disappear.

She studied me as she poured a cup of coffee, handed it to me, and I felt the hairs on the back of my neck prickle. She poured another for Jason before she asked, "Anything else, Mr. Ashby?"

"Yes. Please have Nate take Miss Flynn's bag upstairs to the Rose Bedroom and make a fire there," he said.

We were both silent as she nodded and left. While we sipped coffee, I glanced around the library. Books lined the walls, some so old I knew they must be first editions, and a flat screen TV was built into a space between two bookshelves. Above the fireplace, a brace of dueling pistols bracketed the gold-framed portrait of a stern old man in Confederate uniform. An arched window to one side of the fireplace faced a cracked, empty swimming pool. Opposite the window, French doors led to a flagstone terrace, now rapidly being covered in snow. It was just what I'd envisioned the library of an antebellum house to be, and the coffee service was as well. I sipped my coffee, unsure if I should wait to be offered cake and sandwiches before eating.

As if reading my mind, Jason gestured toward the platters of food. "Please go ahead," he said.

He didn't have to insist. I hadn't had lunch, only a pack of crackers and a can of soda on the train. The sandwiches were pimento cheese, not one of my favorites, but a southern standby. I ate two of the triangles, finished my coffee and poured another cup without being urged. Then I dug into the fruitcake. I know a lot of people make fun of it, but I happen to like it, if it's well made, and that cake definitely was. My hunger may have added a bit to its flavor, but not much.

Mr. Ashby set down his cup, relighted his pipe and studied me with his amber eyes until I felt my face grow hot. Finally he said, "Miss Flynn, I'm afraid I owe you an apology for more than leaving you at the train station. I must say I've brought you here under false pretenses."

My stomach dropped. "There's no job?"

"Oh, no, there's a job, definitely, but perhaps not the one you're expecting. You'll be doing little or no secretarial work, and almost nothing social." He smiled before turning serious. "No, your real duty is to keep my wife alive and as happy as possible. She's … attempted suicide several times, and if I'm to run the farm and see to our investments, I can't watch her every minute." He looked down and to the side, clearly embarrassed by the situation.

13

I felt blindsided, as I stammered, "Shouldn't you get professional help for her? I mean, I'm not really trained for anything like…" I gestured to indicate how big I thought the problem was.

He shook his head with a sad smile. "I got her to a doctor once after she'd slit her wrists and she told him I was trying to kill her and that I'd cut her. She wanted him to call the police so she could bring charges against me." He laughed once, bitterly. "The doctor said if I'd intended to kill her, I'd done a lousy job of it, since it was done with nail scissors and had only nicked a vein. He suggested that she go to the center for abused women for counseling, and I was all for it, but she said if she left Marbury Hill I'd take it away from her. Then he said he'd like to admit her to the hospital for observation, but I couldn't let him do that to her."

It seemed such an obvious thing to do that I was puzzled. "Why not?"

"Her aunt died in a mental institution, and Marian has a horror of that happening to her." He looked down again, the expression of a boy telling tales out of school; it was oddly endearing. "In her last days, the aunt was restrained and raving, and Marian's family thought it would be a good idea to take her to see her aunt. She…"

Jason closed his eyes and shook his head, then focused his gaze on me. "She is terrified of being locked up, but she's clearly not well, and she's a danger to herself. She can get so paranoid she even locks her door to keep me out sometimes. Until the day comes that I can get her to understand that hospitalization can truly be helpful to her, I want her to be as safe and comfortable as possible."

His eyes left mine, and he turned toward the window. "I know what you must be thinking of me, and I deserve every bit of it." He turned back toward me, a puppyish smile on his face. "But before you leave and wash your hands of us, could you at least meet Marian?"

Between my sympathy (and, I'll admit, curiosity) for Marian and the power of that smile, I agreed to meet her. I followed him up the curving staircase that seemed to have no support. At the landing, where the staircase divided into two, he pointed to a half-open door. "That will be your room, between ours. Mine is to the left and Marian's to the right."

He picked up a box that stood on the landing and walked ahead of me to knock on Marian's door.

"It's not locked," came a voice from inside, flat but with a slight edge of impatience.

He turned the crystal knob and pushed open the door. I don't know exactly what I was expecting—a thin, elegant society lady before I'd arrived, or after Jason's description, a wild-eyed lunatic with bandaged wrists—but Marian was neither. She was on the pudgy side, with mousy blond hair that hung to her shoulders. She wore a gold brocade dressing gown that clashed painfully with the pink undertones in her skin. Her eyebrows and eyelashes were the same color as her hair, which made her face look undefined and washed out. However, her eyes were clear and focused, on me, and dark with accusation.

"So this is your girlfriend, Jason," she said. "Hattie told me she was here."

I was too startled to respond, but Jason said, "Marian, honey! You know I don't have any other women in my life and I don't need anyone else. You remember we decided to hire someone to be with you. I told you I interviewed Miss Flynn when I was in Richmond. She's going to be your companion and do whatever you need her to do."

Marian's eyes narrowed. "Don't say 'we' decided, Jason. I had nothing to do with this. You've brought her here to help you get rid of me."

"Marian…" Jason held his hands out toward her pleadingly. "Honey, don't say those things. Ask her yourself why she's here."

She turned to me. "So why are you here? What is your version of the truth? What did he tell you?"

I thought quickly. I dared not tell her that he'd implied she was a danger to herself, but I wanted to show some sympathy for her problems. "He said that you're lonely here. And depressed," I added quickly. "And that you could use some company."

She turned back to her husband. "You don't want to spend any time with me yourself, so you use my money to pay this woman to be my companion. What do we have in common, Miss Flynn? Why do you want to be my companion? Hasn't Jason told you I'm crazy?"

"Well, you know, I may not stay," I said, trying to placate her. "Obviously, I'm here for the night, since it's too late to leave, but afterward, if I decide to stay, it will be on a trial basis. Only as long as you want me here."

That stopped her momentarily. Then she said, "I'm going to call Adam and tell him about this." She reached for a cell phone.

"Don't you remember, hon? Adam's out of town," Jason said, darting a quick glance at me that begged me to remain silent.

I was about to say that Adam had brought me to Marbury Hill, but instead I smiled blandly, wondering what was going on and why Jason was lying to Marian.

"Oh, well, my phone's not charged up anyway, and I've probably run out of minutes." She turned to me. "That's something you can do for me to earn your pay. You can see that my phone stays charged up. I may need to call Adam or someone else." She spied the box and her mood changed. "Oh, you've brought me a gift, Jason!"

"I should have brought you a gift. But it looks like something you ordered from Bell's." He stepped forward and set it down beside her chair.

She frowned in confusion. "I don't remember ordering anything. What is it?"

"Open it and see," he said with a smile that Marian returned. He took out a pocketknife, flicked it open and slid it under the packaging tape.

Marian opened the flaps on the box and drew out a purple and orange striped straw hat, suitable perhaps for sunning on a tropical isle, but quite out of place here at Marbury Hill.

Her smile disappeared, replaced by a look of anger and fear. "I didn't order this! There's been some mistake. I wouldn't buy anything this ugly."

Suddenly, she hurled the hat into the fireplace. It caught fire with a great rush of flame, and a whoosh roared up the chimney.

"Marian! Do you want to set the house on fire?" a scared Jason demanded, grabbing the box back before she could send it to join the now disintegrating hat.

"No," she said petulantly, "but the house is still mine to do with whatever I wish as long as I'm alive."

"And I hope that will be a long time," he said gently.

"Oh, do you? I don't think so," she said, her voice steely and cold, not the voice of a stereotypical raving madwoman but not the voice of someone in the peak of mental health either.

I could think of nothing to say, and began studying the curtains on the far side of the room. Jason decided to let the matter drop, asking Marian, "Do you want to come down to dinner tonight, or shall I have Hattie bring you something on a tray?"

"I'll come down," she said. As Jason and I turned to leave, she called, "Miss Flynn, stay here. You might as well start earning your pay."

I was suddenly nervous to be alone with her. "Could I use the bathroom first?"

She nodded her grudging assent. "You don't need to go to your room or downstairs. You can use mine."

Her bathroom was immaculate, with a marble floor, a pedestal sink and old-fashioned claw-footed tub. Thick monogrammed towels hung on ceramic bars. There were no guest towels, since she didn't expect to have guests, so after I used the toilet and washed my hands, I dried them on one of hers, monogrammed with a double M. Then I took a deep breath and went back into the bedroom.

"What would you like me to do to earn my pay?" I asked more cheerfully than I felt. "I could read to you."

"I'm not a child. I can read." She waved to a stack of books by her bed. "I read for hours."

"Oh. Then we could play cards. I know a few card games, and even chess."

"Card games are a waste of time, and I've wasted a lot on solitaire, but what else do I have to do with my time but waste it?"

"Then what?" I asked. "We can talk."

"About what? Did Jason give you some questions or topics for me?"

"No," I said, starting to feel exasperated. "But maybe he should have, since you don't have anything you want me to do."

She laughed. "Then if you feel useless, you'll know how I feel."

This felt less like the raving of a lunatic than the sadness of a lonely, depressed woman. Adam Carrington had said she had issues, but he'd also said she had good days, and maybe this was one of them.

"Brush my hair," she commanded, so I picked up the brush and began to slide it through her thinning hair, being careful not to pull. She closed her eyes and for a moment I thought she'd fallen asleep. Then she said, "Put my hair up. Do something to make it look nice, and I want some lipstick and eye shadow."

I obliged the best I could. I'm no beautician, and had little to work with, but after a few minutes I thought she looked better. She surveyed herself in the mirror, turning this way and that. "If that's the best you can do, I'll have to settle for it. Jason won't think I'm attractive no matter what. Let's go down to dinner." *This should be fun*, I thought glumly.

Chapter 3

I hadn't noticed the time or heard any bell or gong, but I followed her down the curving staircase and back beyond the library to the dining room.

The dining room could have come from the pages of an upscale magazine. The Ashbys might have neglected the outside of Marbury Hill, but they lived in style. A fire in the big stone fireplace cracked softly, sending golden reflections across the polished floor. Above the table hung a tiered chandelier, its hundreds of crystal prisms sparkling.

But despite the glitter, dinner was about as much fun as I'd feared it would be. Jason sat at one end of a long mahogany table, Marian at the other, and I was halfway between them, so I had to swivel my head from one to the other to attend to their conversation. There was little of it. I was too overwhelmed by the situation at Marbury Hill to care, and I turned my attention to the array of crystal and silver arrayed at each place. I covertly watched the Ashbys to see which piece of silver they used for each course. They might be unhinged or lying, but they did have impeccable table manners.

"Is it still snowing?" Marian asked over the soup course, bowls of lobster bisque with tiny oyster crackers. On our bread plates were hot biscuits and little pats of butter imprinted with a clover pattern.

"It was when I last looked," Jason said.

"Then we should have hot rum punch after dinner," she said.

"Maybe we should just stick with a single glass of wine, honey," he said, lifting his glass as if in a toast.

She took a long drink of her wine, and so did I. It was a good sauterne that went well with the bisque.

"You should let me drink myself into oblivion, Jason," she said. "Then you can carry out your plans."

His shoulders deflated and he frowned with a sigh, but he made no answer. I wondered how often they had this discussion.

When Hattie came to take away the soup plates, I told her how delicious the bisque was. She only nodded. A quiet black teenager, whom I took to be the 'Nate' who'd taken my suitcase upstairs, followed her with a big tray carrying three covered dishes. He set it down and she walked around the table, serving us each slices of rare roast beef, string beans and mashed potatoes with cheese melted on top. As Marian asked for a double serving of the potatoes, Jason said, "I thought you were trying to lose weight."

"Why should I bother? It's not like you care."

They had another confrontation over the wine. Hattie came to Marian first, and started to pour. "I thought we were just going to have the one glass," Jason protested.

"I'm old enough to drink," Marian countered, "and it's my money that's paying for it. Fill my glass, please, Hattie."

I noticed that Hattie had not stopped pouring when Jason spoke up, and I realized that she took her cues from Marian, not Jason. She paused at my place, and I nodded. I wanted to support Marian in her self-assertion, plus the wine was good. Jason didn't tell me not to have more, but he shook his head and smiled at me with comic exasperation. Hattie moved on to refill his glass without his asking, and we three set to eating our main course in silence.

When Hattie and Nate cleared away our plates we sat in awkward silence until she brought in small pecan tarts with whipped cream and steaming cups of coffee. *If I ate like this all the time*, I thought, *I'd be twice Marian's size*. Jason, on the other hand, ate as much as we two did, and was as trim as the day he'd interviewed me. I didn't bother asking if the coffee were decaf. I was so tired and stressed that I was sure I'd fall asleep despite any amount of caffeine.

"Do you think the snow will melt by morning?" I asked.

"Hard to say," Jason said. "It depends on tonight's temperature. I'm afraid you may have to spend an extra day or so here until I can arrange to have the road plowed."

With that bit of discouragement, I said I'd like to go to bed. Marian rose to join me, but Jason poured himself another glass of wine and sat back at the table alone.

At the top of the stairs, I paused at the door of my room. It was ajar. Perhaps Nate had left it that way when he'd made the fire.

Marian touched my arm. "I'm going to lock my door, but if you need to see me, knock and tell me it's you."

"Thank you," I said automatically, wondering why I'd need to see her, and why she'd trust me instead of her husband. "Sleep well."

"I will," she said. "I always take a sleeping pill. But first I'm going to email my cousin Adam about all this."

All what? I wondered. What would she say about me, and what would he make of it?

My room was appropriately named the Rose Bedroom. Thousands of pink roses blossomed on the wallpaper, the bedspread and pillow shams, and on the canopy above the bed. Two plump chairs were upholstered in rose velvet, and matching drapes covered the tall windows. I'd drawn a mental blueprint of the house. My room was in the back, older portion of the mansion, and below it were the dining room and kitchen. The front, newer section crossed it, forming a T.

One of my windows looked across diagonally at Marian's window, the other to Jason's. Someone, probably Nate or Hattie, had loosened the tasseled tiebacks on the drapes so that they hung straight down. I pushed aside the drapes on Marian's side and saw a blur of movement as she crossed her room. She could see into mine as well. I dropped the drape and as I stepped back, Nate stood before me, holding an armload of firewood. He'd come in so silently I hadn't heard him.

"I come to stoke your fire," he said. He went to the fireplace, poked at the embers and added two sticks of wood. The fire spurted and crackled. He stepped back and turned to me, saying quietly, "Please don't do nothing to hurt Miss Marian."

"No, of course I won't," I said, touched by his concern. "Besides, I'll probably be leaving tomorrow."

"Ma'am Hattie don't think so."

I reached for my purse, wondering if I were supposed to tip him, but before I could decide, he slipped out and closed the door behind him.

When I began to unpack, I realized someone had rifled my suitcase. Who? Hattie when she'd gone to tell Marian of my arrival? Nate when he'd made the fire? Marian while Jason and I talked in the library? Even Jason himself had had the opportunity while I was in Marian's room before dinner. But why? Did someone think I'd brought drugs or a weapon? Since Marian thought I'd been hired to spy on her, she might have searched for recording equipment, or sent Hattie to search. Nothing was missing, so whoever had searched had been satisfied with my belongings. I decided that since I'd be leaving the next day there was no need to unpack everything, just my nightgown and robe and toiletries.

I'd had a bath and put on my nightgown and robe, and was creaming my face when there was a tap on my door. Thinking it might be Nate back with more firewood, I opened the door. It was Jason, and seeing me thus, he started with laughter.

"Oh, dear, I'm sorry! I should have come earlier. I just wanted to assure you that you'll be safe if you decide to stay. Marian's moods, as bad as they can be, are temporary. By tomorrow she'll have forgotten she said anything cruel to you or accused you of anything. She's usually more placid and likes to reminisce about the past. I've heard it all," he said, smiling and rolling his eyes slightly. He paused and touched my hand. "She needs you, Kate, and I need you. Please stay."

"I'll think about it," I said. As I stepped back to close the door, I saw movement at Marian's door. She'd been eavesdropping. At least we hadn't done or said anything to be ashamed of, but who knew what she might make of it?

I tossed and turned, thinking about Marian and Jason, and of Adam Carrington, wishing I'd taken his advice. But if I left tomorrow, I'd go back to what? Debts and no job. I'd given up my apartment and put my paltry belongings in storage to take care of Mom. Dad had remarried and moved to Florida, and what little Mom left hadn't even paid her funeral expenses. My sister Joyce and her husband were in graduate school, living in cramped quarters across the continent in California. Having nothing permanent was the main reason Jason Ashby's offer had appealed to me.

Finally I fell asleep, warmed by the fire. I was vaguely aware when the second log broke into and fell, safe behind a firescreen.

I awakened in the night to the sound of sleet. Wind had risen, and I heard the *swish-swish* of ice pellets being blown against the windows. And there was something else: the smell of smoke, an acrid smell that wasn't logs burning. I leapt out of bed, grabbed my robe and shoved my feet into my shoes, the way we'd been taught to do in hotel fire drills. I ran to the window and jerked back the drapes. Flames lit Marian's window, and two figures writhed in the glare like spirits in hell.

By the time I got to Marian's room, the fire was out. One wall was scorched and the blackened remains of drapes littered the floor. The Ashbys stood apart in the midst of the destruction, Jason panting with exertion, Marian staring wide-eyed at him. He dropped the small rug he'd used to beat out the flames. "It's all right now," he said to me. "It's a good thing I was still awake and smelled smoke." He turned to Marian in exasperation and worry. "Honey, you could have burned the house down!"

"Me?" Marian demanded. "Why would I want to burn down Marbury Hill? It's all I have left in the world!"

"You have me," he said, touching her soot-grimed cheek.

She stepped back from him and went on as if he hadn't spoken: "You know, I may leave it to Adam when I die, not to you."

"Why do you keep talking about dying, Marian?" he asked wearily.

"Because I know what you're planning. You don't have to kill me. I'll give you a divorce and I promise not to tell anybody about your—"

He drew her close, pressing her face against his shoulder, cutting off her words. "But Marian, I don't want you dead." He sounded on the verge of tears. "You must be so upset to think such a thing. Look, if you say you didn't start the fire, I believe you. It could have been a spark from the fireplace."

Marian began to sob and he continued talking to her in soothing tones. I turned away and went back to my lonely, chilly room. I slipped under the covers and lay shivering, too frightened to relax. After a while the tense exhaustion of the day overtook me, and I fell asleep.

A tapping on my door awoke me. For a wild moment I couldn't remember where I was, and then it all came whirling back. "Who is it?"

"Hattie, Ma'am. Miss Marian wants you to come down to the dining room and eat with her, and I've set it all out for you. Mr. Ashby say for you to come to the library after you get done with breakfast."

"What time is it? Have I slept past the time for the train?"

"Ain't nobody from here going on a train today. You best look outside."

I did, dismayed. Snow covered everything as far as I could see. It was drifted against the buildings down beyond the house, and piled up on the terrace. The outdoor chairs and benches were rounded heaps of white, and evergreens were laden down with snow and ice, their heavy branches touching the surface of the snow. I was trapped in an icy world, just as Adam had warned me about. "I can't stay here," I protested, my panic rising. "I won't. Mr. Ashby has to take me to the train station,"

"It ain't up to Mr. Ashby," she stated with a rueful smile. "He can't do nothing about the snow anymore than you can or I can. It's like fate done taken a hand. It's intended you should be here." She stepped back from my door and turned toward Marian's room. "I'll be in Miss Marian's room putting up new draperies and cleaning away the mess. I laid out everything for you, and Miss Marian is already downstairs."

I must have looked startled at that, considering what had happened the night before, for

Hattie said. "She feels better today knowing you'll be here."

Looks like I'll be here for a good while, I thought.

Jason had finished breakfast by the time I reached the dining room. Without asking, Hattie had poached eggs, baked biscuits for us and poured juice and coffee. I expected Marian to say something about the fire, but she didn't. She acted the good hostess, offering me extra coffee, passing the silver pot of strawberry jam, just as if I were a college friend visiting for the weekend. Had she blocked out the fire? I started to mention it, but decided to wait for her or Jason to bring it up.

"Isn't it beautiful outside, Kate?" Marian said, pushing back from the table to go to the big window. "It's just the way I remember it was when I was a child, and my father put me on a sled and pulled me all around the front lawn. He taught me to ski later when I was a teenager, but I was never good at it. Maybe you and I can ski or we can go to the storage house and find my old sled. We even used to have a sleigh pulled by horses, but the riding horses aren't good at pulling sleighs. When the snow melts we can go riding."

I tried to join in her excitement, but after last night's accusations and fire, I felt more unnerved than delighted. I couldn't help thinking some of it must be fantasy, and when the snow melted I planned to be long gone, no matter what Hattie said about fate.

We took our coffee to the library where Jason had tuned the TV to the weather channel. Bad news poured fourth: schools, businesses and day care centers closed, meetings canceled, roads treacherous. No one was to go out unless it was an emergency. There were the usual scenes of cars sliding on icy roads, stranded people sleeping on the floor of airports, and news of a family of three who had died from carbon monoxide poisoning due to a space heater. The whole of southern Virginia—and indeed the whole East Coast—had come to a standstill, and my life with it.

Chapter 4

And yet, I felt strangely safe, despite the events of the night before. The accidents and fires, while tragic, seemed far away from Marbury Hill, especially because the electricity stayed on. I had a feeling of suspended animation, as if we were all waiting for a mass of snow to slide off the roof, or icicles to snap and crash. An eerie stillness hung over everything and we were connected to the outside world only by thin wires. What if we'd needed the fire department, or an ambulance?

The sun came out about nine that morning and the sky turned from gray to a vivid unclouded blue. Marian had been staring at the TV screen as I had, scarcely seeing what was passing before us. I realized we'd seen the same loop of news several times. Suddenly she set down her empty coffee cup and stood. "I know what: let's go out and make a snowman, Kate. Jason too."

"A snowman?" he said laughing, and I saw the disappointment take over her face.

I didn't want to see another argument erupt over nothing. "I think that would be fun," I said, putting down my own cup. "I'll go with you. But I don't have any boots."

"We can probably find some for you in my mother's room," she said. "She had small feet like yours."

Jason stood as if to object, then shrugged and sank back into his chair.

Marian headed upstairs and I followed. We met Hattie coming down, and when Marian said what she wanted, Hattie turned and went with us. As we passed the door to Marian's bedroom, the smell of smoke still hung in the air, and I wanted to turn back, remembering. I saw that there were two more bedrooms to the front of the house beyond Marian's and Jason's. From deep in the pocket of her dress Hattie drew out a string of keys and unlocked the door on the right. A faint fragrance of lilac wafted out.

I followed the two into what appeared to be a shrine to Marian's mother. The bed was made with a lavender silken coverlet and satin sheets were turned back from the pillow, just as if someone would soon be getting in bed. A lace-trimmed negligee lay across one pillow. On the dresser various bottles of perfume and jars of cream were neatly arranged beside a hairbrush and makeup mirror. There wasn't a speck of dust anywhere, and I knew without going into the bathroom that it too would be just as it had been the last time its occupant had used it.

Marian slid open the door to a walk-in closet and by this time I was prepared for what I saw: racks of dresses, suits, coats, slacks and blouses hung in perfect order, by color. Plastic drawers lining the wall held jewelry and neatly folded items that I knew would be lingerie and sweaters, scarves and gloves. Below were more boxes, full of shoes. Marian pulled out one and handed me a pair of tall, polished leather boots.

"They ain't for snow, Miss Marian. They for riding horses," Hattie gently objected.

"Oh," Marian said. She put them back, pulled out another plastic drawer and came up with a pair of high-heeled boots of a rubbery material trimmed around the top with a cuff of fur. I sat down in one of the velvet-covered chairs, careful not to muss anything, and pulled on the boots. To my astonishment, they fit.

"See, I was right!" Marian crowed. "You're so much like my mother I just knew they would fit. Put on one of her sweaters too if you want." She slid open an upper drawer and pulled out a Scandinavian style ski sweater.

"Oh, but I have sweaters—and a coat," I objected.

"A parka would be better for out in the snow." She took a quilted down-filled parka off a hanger and handed it to me. I decided to wear it, since my coat was a little dressy for making a snowman. "Do I really look like your mother?"

She nodded, but behind her Hattie was shaking her head.

"Let's lock up, Miss Marian, so nothing happens to Miss Olivia's things." Hattie urged us out, locked the door behind her and pocketed the key.

In my room I glanced around for my suitcase. It was missing from the luggage rack where I'd left it. I opened the closet and saw that my clothing had been neatly hung and the suitcase zipped closed and stowed below the racks. Surely Hattie had done this, but when? It was clear that she meant me to stay.

Back downstairs, Marian called eagerly, "Out this way, Kate. We can make our snowman in the front lawn and then walk around the house and down to the stable and storage houses."

"Oh, what are you doing at the stable?" Jason asked, joining us.

"I want to show Jeff to Kate." She turned to me. "Jeff is short for Jefferson

Davis, my horse. He's a trained jumper, and a much better horse than Jason's."

She ignored his furrowed brow, but I couldn't help noticing. It seemed like he didn't want us to go outside or to the stable. "I'm not sure that's safe. The men haven't shoveled the path to the stable yet," he objected.

"It's all right. We're wearing boots, and it's more fun to walk in snow instead of a path."

He followed us out onto the front porch with an uneasy smile, and as Marian ran forward, flung herself into the snow and began to make a snow angel, he snapped a photo of her. I wondered why, but she didn't object, so I said nothing.

"Come on, Kate, you too!" she said.

Feeling a little foolish, I dropped down into the snow and moved my own legs and arms to make a pattern. Then we stood up, laughing and brushing the snow off ourselves. Marian bent, scooped up a handful of snow, squeezed it tight and hurled it at Jason, striking him squarely in the face.

Jason's expression went blank and I thought I felt a split-second jolt of rage from him, but it disappeared almost immediately as he laughingly scolded "Honey!" and went inside, shaking his head.

Marian looked after him as he closed the door. "He'll make me pay for that, but it was worth it," she murmured. "So how do we start making a snowman, Kate?" she asked, turning to me. "I've forgotten!"

I gathered snow into a ball and began rolling it to pick up more snow. After it got too heavy for us to push further, we set it up to be the base and began to roll the second segment. After a few minutes our snowman had a body and snow arms pressed onto his sides, but he lacked facial features or a hat. It didn't seem to bother Marian. "He's a fine snowman," she announced. "Now, let's go to the stable." She took my hand and led the way around the house. As we passed by the library window, I saw Jason watching us. He looked disappointed, but I couldn't tell if the object of such disappointment were Marian or me. Perhaps we both were.

The snow was deeper away from the house, and we were gasping for breath, making little puffs of steam in the air, by the time we'd floundered down the lane to the stable.

The door stood ajar, and as we went in and my eyes adjusted to the gloom, I saw a man tearing open a bale of hay, distributing it into the long wooden trough that ran across in front of three stalls. He turned when he saw us. "Miss Marian, what you doing out in the snow? I haven't seen you since Hector was a pup."

"I'm feeling better than I've felt since Hector was a pup," she said, going along with his idiom. "I brought my friend Kate to see Jeff. Is he okay, Lucas?"

"Course he is, Miss Marian. You know I'll take good care of him so you needn't worry about him. I think he's missed you, though, haven't you, Jeff?"

The big red horse snuffled and pawed the straw-covered earth in his stall. I said a silent prayer that he would recognize Marian and show her some affection. After a moment he pushed his head through the stanchions holding up the floor above and rubbed his head against her hand. She laid her head against his, and stripped off her gloves so he could sniff her hand. If he'd been a cat, he'd have been purring, and so would Marian.

"Jeff, my beautiful boy," she crooned. "When this snow melts we're going to ride again. You'd like that, wouldn't you?"

He tossed his head and whinnied, as if to agree with her. With a last caress of his nose, she pulled on her glove and turned to the other stall. There a larger black horse stood eating hay. He raised his head to look at her and when she reached to pet him, he backed away. "He's Jason's horse," she said. "Jason's trained him to dislike me, but maybe he'll like you, Kate."

I doubted it, but I put out my own hand. The horse sniffed at it then took a step back and returned to his hay.

"Let's go up into the loft," Marian said.

"You be careful, Miss Marian. The steps need some fixing. If you're not careful you could slip. It's been a long time since you went up there."

"Kate can hold my hand," she said, and reached for me, doubling my own anxiety over old rickety barn steps that needed fixing.

As we started up, it was so dark I could hardly make my own way, much less take care of her, but after a few steps we reached the upper floor and she pushed open wooden shutters at the end of the loft. Light flooded in and she walked around, pushing at bales of hay.

"It's not here," she announced. "My sled's not here. Jason must have thrown it away."

"Then let's go back down," I said. Something about it gave me the creeps. "You go ahead. I'll close the shutters after you're all the way down, so you can see where you're walking."

She did as I suggested, but still I heard her miss a step and fall forward, catching herself against the side of the staircase. I closed the shutters and felt my own way down.

Lucas was still in the stable. "Why'd you want to go up there, Miss Marian? I told you it was unsafe." He didn't seem to be scolding her, just puzzled.

"It's not there," she said. "My sled is gone."

"Nothing up there but hay," he said. "That's all I remember being up there."

"I used to have a sled, a Red Racer," she said. "Kate was going to pull me in it."

"I never saw any sled up there as long as I've worked here for Mr. Ashby," he said.

Marian said nothing, but went to Jeff's stall and gave him one more caress before saying, "Come on, Kate."

As we went back into the blinding snow-reflecting sunshine, she fumed, "Jason's thrown it away. I know he has. He doesn't want me to have anything of my own."

As we approached the house, I saw Hattie out in a secluded spot where the sun hadn't touched, scooping up virgin snow into a plastic dishpan. "Oh, we're going to have snow ice cream," Marian cried.

And so we did. For lunch we had our dessert first. Hattie had made snow ice cream the way I too remembered from childhood visits to my grandparents: a mixture of sugar, vanilla and coffee cream stirred into snow. It was a bit thin and icy, as it always was, but it tasted delicious. Jason didn't finish his, joking about waiting for the cookie dough flavor, but Marian and I polished off huge servings, and she insisted that Nate be allowed to come in and eat some as well.

Only afterward did we have toasted pimento cheese sandwiches, their outsides crusty with browned butter, and strangely enough, turnip greens with bits of ham and cooked turnip. It was an unusual dinner by most standards, but Marian thanked Hattie over and over for making a winter lunch like she remembered. Jason asked for a ham sandwich and a cup of coffee.

Marian waited until we'd finished eating before she turned to Jason. "I had a sled in the loft over the stable, and now it's gone."

"I'll go take a look this afternoon," he said.

"I looked," she said. "Have you taken it away?"

"Of course not, honey; I don't need a sled! Perhaps Lucas may have thrown some hay over it," he suggested.

"He said he hadn't seen it," she protested.

"Well, I'll go down and take a look. If the sled's gone, we'll just get you a new one."

"By that time the snow will have melted," she said, starting to frown. "And I don't want any old sled. I want that one."

"Okay, honey," he said wearily. He pushed back his chair and left the table; in a few minutes we heard the back door close, slightly louder than usual.

Marian turned to me, touching my hand where it lay on the table. "Kate, this was the happiest day I've had in a long time—until Jason ruined it."

I didn't know what to say, but I appreciated her overture of friendship. I turned my hand over, palm up, and squeezed hers.

"You look so much like my mother, and you're kind. Do you mind if I consider you my mother?"

That startled me. Marian was older than I, and I didn't in any way think of myself as her mother. True I'd worn her mother's boots and parka, both of which now rested in racks in a back hallway off the kitchen.

"I mean, just pretend," Marian said, seeming to realize that she might have gone too far.

"If it makes you feel better, sure," I said, and managed a smile. I silently vowed to myself to leave as soon as I could.

We went in the library where I turned on the TV and settled back in a chair by the fireplace to watch. Marian stood behind my chair, her hand on my shoulder. I found it disconcerting, but managed to focus on the news. More snow was predicted for the late afternoon and night, with dropping temperatures, and icing over areas that had melted in the sunlight today. It was discouraging news.

Jason came back in, stomping the snow off his shoes onto the carpet, and rubbing his hands together briskly. "The sled's right where I said it would be," he declared. "I don't know how you missed it. Come on and I'll show you."

"You come too, Kate, please," she said. I'd decided before she asked that I'd go. I wanted to see the sled that was causing so much trouble.

Jason opened the stable door and strode past the three horse stalls to the staircase. He took Marian's hand and half dragged her up the steps. At the top he opened the shutters and pointed. "See? There it is!" he said.

I was a few steps behind Marian, and there was no mistaking a red sled lying against a hay bale.

"It wasn't there this morning," Marian said. "Did you see it then, Kate?"

"No," I said, thoroughly confused.

"Well, it's here now," Jason said with a shrug and a smile. He picked it up and went over to close the shutters. "You girls go on down. I'll bring it the sled," he called.

I went ahead, eager to get out of the stable. Marian came after me, half stumbling. "It wasn't there," she kept repeating. When Jason set the sled down in the snow outside, she walked all around it. "That's not the one I had."

"Well, it's the one that's been stored in the stable," he protested, spreading his hands in a here-you-go gesture. "If it's not the one you had, where do you think this one came from? Sleds don't just appear out of nowhere," he said laughing.

"I don't know," Marian murmured. Her face was creased with confusion.

"Get on," I said, eager to break the impasse. "I'll pull you back to the house, and we can put the sled in the back hall near the kitchen where Hattie can keep an eye on it. Maybe Nate would like to take a ride on it."

She smiled and climbed on, holding to the sides. I took hold of the rope and tugged, but she was heavy. Jason gave a push from behind to get the sled moving, and together we struggled up the hill toward the house with our child-woman passenger.

That afternoon we three sat in the library by the fire, each reading and occasionally checking the news on TV. Jason found a football game and turned the sound down so we wouldn't be disturbed. I found a book on Civil War history, and Marian went upstairs for a romance she'd been reading.

When she was out of earshot, Jason said, "You see what I meant about her moods changing. Has she said anything strange to you?"

I shook my head. I wasn't about to tell him she considered me her mother, and I didn't know who was right about the sled. I certainly hadn't seen it when Marian and I had gone to the stable in the morning. Had Jason moved some hay to expose it? Or had he found it somewhere else and put it there to confuse her? And if so, why?

I was glad when dinner was over and it was time for me to go to bed. I took the book up to my room, which was warmed by a fire tended by the conscientious Nate. I left the borrowed boots and parka downstairs. Tomorrow I'd wear my own clothes, I promised myself.

Chapter 5

I lingered over the breakfast tray Hattie brought me as long as I could, savoring my solitude, postponing my confrontation with the Ashbys. Hattie's food and my lovely warm bedroom would be things I'd miss when I finally left Marbury Hill. I poured the last of the coffee into my cup and saucer and went to stand at the window facing Marian's. There was no sign of life from her window. Was she asleep, or already downstairs planning something petty, childish or just plain weird? Our snowman was out on the front lawn, so I couldn't see it from my room, but I could see the garden, a frozen fairyland. I wondered what it would look like in springtime, when the snow had melted, then reminded myself that I wouldn't be here to see it.

I pulled on slacks and a sweater and went down to the library. Jason was writing at a big rolltop desk. He closed his ledger and turned to me, his smile almost triumphant. "Well, Miss Flynn, for your sake I'm sorry you're marooned here for yet another day, but for our sake, I'm glad."

"How soon can I leave?"

My bluntness clearly startled him. "Well, I suppose in another two or three days. It all depends on the weather. We're not prepared for snow here. I've called around to locate a private snowplow service to clear our driveway. Lucas or one of the tenants will shovel the paths to the outbuildings in case Marian wants to go see that beloved old horse of hers."

"Ah, okay. That makes sense," I said lamely, feeling a touch of guilt for being so obvious about wanting to leave.

Jason stood and walked over to poke at the fire, then turned back to me. "Since you're stuck here, why not go up and amuse Marian? I'll pay you for however many days you spend here."

"How will I find her this morning?" I asked with some unease.

"Do you mean where, or in what emotional state? The answer to the where is her room. You know, Hattie is a miracle-worker; you can barely smell the smoke anymore. As to her condition, I have no idea. We have separate rooms and I haven't seen or talked with her this morning." He walked over to me and lowered his voice. "Will you let me know how she is, if there's anything ... especially unusual about her today?"

I agreed, though I felt uncomfortable about it. On the one hand, I was being put in the position of spy, but on the other hand, I'd already held back some things I might have told him. And he was, after all, the one who had hired me.

When I tapped on Marian's door she opened it immediately. When she saw me, her smile faded. "Have you seen Jason this morning?"

"Yes. I just came from the library."

Hattie was behind Marian, making the bed. She finished, picked up Marian's breakfast tray and went out.

"What did he say?" Marian asked.

"He said that because we had more snow last night it could be another three days before I can leave." I stood awkwardly, waiting for her to welcome me in, offer me a seat or give me some hint as to what to do.

"Three days," she repeated. "What else?"

"He said, 'Go and amuse Marian.'"

She scoffed. "That will be difficult unless we go out in the snow again. I don't find much in my life amusing. We can play cards." She sat down at a small mahogany table and picked up a deck of cards, idly dealing out a hand of Solitaire. "Move that chair over here."

I moved the chair she indicated to the table, facing her, and sat down. She regarded me with gray eyes, so pale they seemed to fade, like a cloud that disappears up close.

"Do you feel uneasy being this close to a crazy person?"

I started to say that she seemed sane, but the words stuck in my throat. Was it crazy to call someone younger your mother? Was it crazy to forget ordering something and then toss it into the fire instead of returning it?

"I'm sure Jason told you I'm crazy." When I neither agreed nor denied it, she went on, "He's trying to drive me insane and some days I think he's succeeded. He has all the advantages. He's made me a prisoner in my own home, and I have nothing to do, no purpose. If I sit quietly, he says I'm being apathetic, even catatonic. If I get angry, he accuses me of being hysterical." She smiled. "Hysterical is a lot more fun." She picked up a card and placed it atop the correct one. "I hate Jason."

"Why don't you get a divorce?"

"How? He won't let me leave. I tried calling a lawyer, but he took away the phone and told the lawyer I was off my medication and didn't know what I was saying." She looked at me with tears starting to well in her eyes. "Will you help me escape, Mother?"

"Marian, I'd really prefer it if you didn't call me mother, even if you're pretending. That… that's one of those things that might make someone who overheard it think you were crazy."

She turned back to her cards and went on as if she hadn't heard me. "I promised Jason I would never tell his secret, but he doesn't believe me. Who would I tell? I can't go anywhere and no one comes here to see me except once in a while my cousin Adam. He doesn't like Jason, and he told me I was crazy to marry Jason in the first place."

She slapped down the remaining cards and gripped my arm, piercing me with a gaze that shocked me. Why had I thought her eyes were pale? They were commanding. "If I can't leave when you do, will you take my box to Adam?"

"What? What kind of box?"

She flung open her closet door, rummaged behind clothes and held up a child's carved wooden chest with a curved, decorated top. It smelled slightly of spices, and had a shiny brass padlock. As I reached for it, she pulled it back. "I'll give it to you just before you leave," she announced, and hid the box away once more. "Jason must never get it. He'd destroy it."

"What's in it?" I pictured a variety of contents, from jewels to children's toys to safety pins; anything could be in there, knowing Marian.

"The truth. The story of my past, and of what happened with Jason. Adam's the only one left of my family, and he'll know what to do with the box. He'll see that justice is done, but he's not to open it until after I'm dead."

Here we go again, I thought. "Marian," I said as gently as I could, "you must stop talking about your death. "

"But I can't! I've had a premonition that my death is not far off. Jason's determined to kill me. Do you want proof that I'm crazy? Even knowing what I know about him, I still love him." She threw back her head and laughed, an eerie laugh that chilled me in spite of the warm fire crackling in the fireplace beside us. It wasn't just the laugh that was chilling; it was the realization that Marian was so obsessed with her own death, she had decided that it was a foregone conclusion. Had she decided to take matters into her own hands?

"You know, your husband hired me to protect you," I said.

"Protect me? From whom? Oh, I get it: to keep me from killing myself. Isn't that what he told you?"

Reluctantly, I nodded.

"I have thought of killing myself," she admitted. "I have so little to live for." She brought her face close to mine, her eyes now a hard gray like burnished metal. "Have you ever thought of killing yourself, Kate?"

I thought for a moment of how hopeless my life had seemed when Harold had broken up with me, when I'd sobbed myself to sleep each night. "Yes, briefly," I admitted. "But I didn't go through with it."

"No kidding," she said drily. "Neither did I."

I was trying to think up a response to that when Hattie tapped on the door and came back in. "Will you be okay without me, Miss Marian?" she asked, glancing pointedly at me.

"Yes, Hattie, I'm fine today. Miss Flynn will look after me, and we'll come down to lunch, and maybe we'll even go out in the snow again."

Hattie nodded, satisfied, and closed the door. In a moment I heard the door to my bedroom open and close, and I knew she was taking my tray down. She'd have no further excuse to check on us.

Suddenly Marian grabbed my arm, leaned forward and whispered, "Jason has killed before. Everybody thought she fell and hit her head, but he pushed her. I saw it, but I didn't move to help her, even when I heard her scream."

"*What?*" This was out of left field. "Who was this? When did it happen?"

"I can't tell you any more about it. You're probably going to report everything I say to Jason, and if you know too much, he'll have to kill you too."

"Hang on, Marian, that's … you shouldn't say stuff like that."

"All right," she said with a shrug. "Tell me all about yourself."

My mind reeled with the effort to follow her abrupt switches of thought. I felt like an earthbound creature trying to follow a bird that flitted from treetop to treetop. "What would you like to know?"

"Why aren't you married?" I must have been getting used to Marian's whiplash style of conversation, because this question didn't bother me as much as it usually did when asked by an acquaintance.

"I was engaged; it didn't work out. It was pretty rough for a while there, but I figure I'm bound to find the right man someday."

"Of course you will. You're young and pretty. That's what men want. It's the ugly ones like me who have trouble finding somebody to love them."

"Marian, stop that! You're not ugly. You have a great bone structure and lovely eyes."

She shrugged off my compliment. "Have you noticed Jason's eyes?"

Only the second I met him, I thought. "They're very unusual."

Marian flew out of her chair. "So, you have been looking at him! I knew it: you're here to take him away from me. Now I know I can't trust you any more than I trust him." She turned away from me and started to cry. "I'm a fool. I had begun to like you. I even wanted to hug you as if you were my mother."

"No, no, no, I don't want your husband!" I protested. "I just want the snow to melt so I can leave this place before I go crazy myself." I started for the door.

She grabbed my arm to pull me back. "No, wait, Kate. I'm sorry I said that. I want you to stay. I need you to talk to. Jason never talks to me anymore."

Can you blame him? I thought, but I didn't leave.

"What would you like to talk about, Kate?" she asked, as though I were the one who'd suggested we talk.

Racking my brains for a subject that wouldn't incite any further mood swings, I glanced around at her room, noting the crown molding, the plaster ceiling medallion, the reeded mantel above the fireplace and the antique cherry furniture. Her bed was spread with a puffy comforter and pink satin sheets. The room was totally feminine. "You have a lovely room."

"It was Aunt Varina's room. After the tragedy it was closed off for a long time. Then my mother said the superstitions about it were silly, and she had it opened up and redecorated just for me. Marbury Hill was so beautiful then, but Jason has let things go. Come and look at the view, Kate." She led me to the tall window that obliquely faced mine, as I worried that even her room's décor had the potential to be an explosive topic.

I looked down on the patio, the garden, clusters of buildings with red metal roofs and a dark forest, all mantled in white. As I looked a mass of snow broke free from the stable roof and slid down to crash and pile up below. *Perhaps we could talk about snow*, I thought. *That should be innocuous enough…*

"Can you see the river, Kate?" I looked where she pointed, and through the woods I saw the silvery gleam of water. "I used to dream that a knight would sail up the river and rescue me. Not that I needed or wanted to be rescued from my parents, but from… regular life." That was something I could definitely relate to.

"One day I managed to hole up in the attic and climb through one of those dormer windows onto the roof. I tied a red scarf to the chimney as a signal to my knight, but the next time I rode to the river I looked back and I couldn't even see my scarf. Besides, the river is too shallow here for boats." She laughed and went on. "Then I decided my hero would have an accident in the woods and I would nurse him back to health and he'd love me forever. But deep down I knew that was just a silly dream too. Nobody ever came here except for salesmen and people we already knew, friends of my parents, and they didn't have handsome sons to love me. They had pretty little girls that made me feel big and awkward, or mean little boys that threw rocks at the horses and cows. Adam was the only nice man who came. Did I tell you about Adam?"

"Only that he's your cousin and that you want me to take your box to him." I left the after-death part out.

"Maybe," she said with a slight frown. "I'm not sure I can trust you not to give it to Jason."

She'd broken out of her dreamlike story of heroes, and we were back to what passed for present reality. "How did you meet Jason?" I asked. Surely he hadn't had an accident in the woods at Marbury Hill.

"On a ship. It was very romantic."

"Tell me about it," I said, eager to find a happy subject.

"Some other time. Right now I want to tell you about Adam. He came to see me at boarding school. I told everybody he was my fiancé on his way to Africa. I didn't have any friends and I hated school. But I hated it here too. My mother was so beautiful, and I wasn't. I used to pray that I'd look like her, but each time I saw myself in the mirror, I always looked the same. Then when she died—"

She stopped and seemed to shake herself to get rid of a bad memory. I had a memory of my own, of her saying I looked like her mother, insisting I wear her mother's clothing, wanting to pretend I was her mother. I felt trapped, not just by the snow, but by Marian's fantasies.

"We had a beach cottage, on the ocean. When I was eighteen I fell in love with the lifeguard that patrolled our part of the beach. I swam out where I knew it was dangerous, so he'd have to rescue me. We dated, and I was overjoyed when he asked me to marry him."

"Why didn't you?"

"My father paid him to go away. That's what he'd wanted all along, money, not me."

Just hearing her say it, I felt a little of the heartbreak she must have experienced at such a young age. I wanted to give her a hug and console her, but nothing I could do or say would change the awful, lonely childhood she'd had. Still, I tried: "What did you enjoy most when you were a child?"

"Riding. Father would never let me try the highest jumps, for fear I'd hurt myself. Now it wouldn't make any difference, not even if I killed myself. I'd like to get on Jeff and take the jump down the lane. At least I'd have one moment of pure joy, soaring through the air, free from the earth."

She looked enthralled by her vision, then her face crumpled as she said, "What's the use? My dreams never come true. Only once I got what I wanted, and that was Jason, but that's turned out terribly wrong. It's too late for me."

She turned away from the window and picked up a paperback novel she'd left on the bedside table. She thrust it at me. "Here, read to me. At least in books dreams come true."

It was such a relief to have a task that was clearer and easier than trying to keep up with Marian's thoughts and say appropriate things in response. I read to her about a lovely maiden rescued by a brave knight who fought off an evil rival who'd kidnapped her and took her to a castle with shining white walls. When I saw that she'd fallen asleep, I closed the book and went downstairs.

Chapter 6

When I went into the library to report that Marian was sleeping, Jason asked, "Did she take sleeping pills?"

"Not while I was there."

Hattie was in the library with Jason; he asked her if she'd given Marian anything, but Hattie shook her head.

"I was just asking Hattie to bring our lunch in here so we don't have to make a fire in the dining room," he said to me.

"Not much trouble making a fire," Hattie said. "It'd give Nate something to do. Or I could take a tray upstairs for you, Miss Flynn, when I take Miss Marian's." It was clear that she didn't want Jason and me alone together.

"I'll do whatever's easiest for you," I said. Hattie would be a good ally to have in this house, even if it were just for the next two or three days.

"We'll have lunch here," Jason announced.

She nodded and went out without a further word, her back stiff with disapproval.

"She'll be back several times, ostensibly to ask if everything is all right, but actually to chaperone us," Jason said.

So he'd interpreted her meaning too. We both chuckled, and I realized it was the first time I'd laughed at Marbury Hill.

Moments later, Hattie brought in a simple lunch of soup and sandwiches. The food looked delicious, and I told her so. She responded with a look that said she knew I was trying to get on her good side, and she didn't anticipate me having much success.

After Hattie left the room, Jason got right to the point. "How did things go this morning?" he asked, his amber eyes on me. They weren't sparkling with gold flecks now; they were filled with worry, and I wished I could say something to set Jason at ease.

"Marian talked … a lot."

"About what?"

"A dozen topics. I was dizzy and confused at the way she skipped from one subject to another. But she kept coming back to death. She's obsessed by it." It seemed strange to be discussing death while we spooned Hattie's delicious cheddar cheese soup.

"Does she still claim I'm trying to kill her?" he asked wearily.

I hesitated. I was sure Hattie was nearby, listening and waiting to report back to Marian. "Yes, she did. But mostly she talked about her childhood."

"The knight, the lifeguard, the beautiful mother?"

I nodded.

"Poor Marian," he said. "The same old stories. I'm glad she has a new listener. Is that all she talked about?"

I wondered if there was something specific Jason was worried about Marian telling him. The two of them talked about each other so much, but only rarely talked *to* each other, and clearly neither of them trusted the other. For now, I'd do well to be wary of them both. I kept my voice casual and gave a slight shrug. "Yes. I spent most of the morning reading to her from a historical romance, *Only the Heart Has Answers.*"

"How does it end?"

"Happily, of course. It wouldn't be much of a romance if it didn't!" I laughed at my own joke.

"Pure fantasy, like everything she talks about," he said, shaking his head.

I ate silently, not meeting his gaze for fear he would detect something from my expression. *He knows I'm holding something back,* I thought. *I've got to be more careful when I'm around him.*

"Kate, are you … are you worried about something? You seem tense."

"Hm? Oh, no."

"You're not afraid of me, are you?" he chuckled.

"No, of course not!" It wasn't fear I felt, but something else, something that combined feeling like a fool when I spoke to him, wanting his eyes to twinkle at me and not quite trusting him… or myself.

"Of Marian?"

"No. I feel sorry for her." That was the complete truth.

"Then stay and be her friend. She needs you. We both do." He finished his coffee and lemon pie, and stood. "Like to go for a walk in the snow?"

"Yes, if you'll wait until I can get Marian ready."

"No," he said with a laugh. "I'm not inviting her. I want to get to know you better."

My pulse quickened slightly. "What do you want to know? I'm just an ordinary person."

"I know why I wanted you to come here, but not why you were willing to come. And I need to know how to persuade you to stay." The eyes were twinkling again.

"I needed a job. Simple enough," I said with a shrug. "I have debts, your pay was good."

"'Was'? Oh dear, that's in the past tense. If you were planning to stay, you'd have said my pay 'is' good."

I nodded. "Well, I'm still not decided. It depends on events. "

"I know you aren't running from the law," he said. "I checked."

"If I were, I'd run to the Caribbean instead of to a snowbound plantation!" I said, trying to turn the conversation light. Of course he'd investigated me, but I hadn't investigated him. I realized that I didn't know any more about him or Marian than what each of them had told me, and I didn't know how much of that to believe. I glanced back at the house and said, "I'll go check on Marian. She's probably awake and ready for lunch and a few more chapters of the romance."

"Another time, then," he said, disappointment clear in his voice.

As I headed upstairs, I couldn't help wondering why he had wanted to walk in the snow with me. Why couldn't he have asked or said whatever he wanted right there in the library?

I spent the next few days with Marian, doing her hair and nails, raising the hemlines on some of her dowdiest outfits, and reading her a seemingly endless series of romances, all so alike that I scarcely knew where we'd left off reading except for the markers. Our conversations were light and impersonal. She never again referred to her "secret" of that snowy morning, and I was glad that she didn't. As the snow melted, one day blurred into another, and I was lulled by the gracious style of life at Marbury Hill so that I began to believe that everything would stay serene. I should have known better.

During those few days, we saw Jason only at dinner, and afterward the three of us played cards or watched TV. We were like three strangers staying at an off-season hotel, sharing food and lodging but not our thoughts.

One night as Marian and I came down to dinner, Jason greeted her with, "Marian, you look especially lovely tonight." I had to agree; I had spent half an hour showing her how to define her brows with a very gentle application of brown mascara, and the difference was noticeable.

"You needn't bother with compliments, Jason," Marian returned. "What do you want from me?"

Be nice, Marian, I willed her silently. *He's making an effort. Meet him halfway.*

Jason tried again. "Is it an offense for a man to tell his wife her hair looks very nice done up that way and that the blue dress has always been one of my favorites? If so, I plead guilty. I think having Miss Flynn here is good for you."

She glanced sharply at me, as if to ask if I'd put him up to complimenting her, but I smiled and shook my head slightly. That seemed to relax her; she smiled at him and glowed with pleasure.

His compliments grew more flowery each night until I began to feel a bit embarrassed in their presence and started to wonder what he was intending. But once Marian had been cajoled into believing the first few compliments, she never questioned further.

Jason never looked at me during dinner or spoke to me except to ask each evening, "How did things go today?"

I got a little bored with his asking the same thing repeatedly, as I had nothing to report. He and I were never alone, so Marian's jealousy subsided until one morning she squeezed my hand and said, "Kate, I'm glad Jason brought you here, though I wasn't glad at first. Please stay."

I never made a conscious decision to stay at Marbury Hill, but by the time the snow melted, the pattern had been set, and I stayed.

One day after lunch when I went to her room for our usual routine, she surprised me by announcing, "I've invited my cousin Adam for supper tonight. You'll like him."

I should have said, "I've already met him," but it was too late for that without a lot of explanation and apology. I'd listened to her talk about him as if I had no idea who he was and it was too late to go back and explain. Now I asked, "Does Jason know?"

"Not yet, but he doesn't have to. Jason doesn't like him, but I'm the hostess and I can invite whomever I want to. I told Hattie, and she'll fix his favorite foods."

I hadn't especially liked Adam Carrington when he'd brought me to Marbury Hill, but I wanted him to see that I'd managed here despite his warnings. And it would be a treat to see someone besides the Ashbys for a change. Maybe I could at least warn him not to mention that he'd brought me to Marbury Hill. Jason knew, but Marian had never asked how I arrived. My opportunity to call Adam came when Marian went down to tell Hattie to expect a guest for dinner. I found Adam's number and dialed, but I had only one bar of service and a nearly dead charge on my cell. I'd neglected to keep it charged, and I got only a buzzing sound from the other end.

"I want you to give my hair some extra attention," Marian said, seating herself in front of her triple mirror. "I'll wear the blue dress. Jason always says it looks good on me, and Adam will probably compliment me on it too—and that'll make Jason jealous," she added with a giggle.

"But he's your cousin," I said, puzzled. "Why would Jason be jealous?"

"Jason doesn't want me to have a relationship with anyone but him. You'll see. He may even turn against you now that I like you."

I didn't want to think too much about that statement, though I wondered if it were Marian's usual manipulations or if she were speaking from experience.

I had Marian's hair and makeup done in plenty of time, but I had to rush with my own appearance. I regretted not accepting Marian's offer of her mother's sweaters. They were finer than mine, a lot of them soft cashmeres. I settled on navy wool slacks and an apricot sweater, although Marian was wearing a dress and she'd probably have Jason don something special. Still, I was the 'hired help,' so to speak, and thus wasn't expected to dress up like the host and hostess. Besides, I neither needed nor wanted to impress Adam Carrington.

I intended to speak to see him before Marian did, to warn him to pretend to be just meeting me, but as I came downstairs I saw Marian leading him into the library, her voice lively with excitement.

I hurried downstairs and went into the library just as he said, "I'm glad you invited me, Marian, and it's good to see you again too, Jason. I was getting a little stir-crazy snowed in over at the cabin. You were lucky to reach me today, Marian. Half the time my phone has been out of order, or maybe the weather has brought down lines and taken out satellite signals."

He turned when I went into the library, and his smile made me feel warm all over. "Well, Miss Flynn, it looks as if you're thriving here."

"How do you know her name?" Marian demanded. "I didn't tell you."

Before I could signal him, he said, "Well I did bring her here from the station."

It took a few seconds for Marian to connect all the dots. Then she turned to Jason, her eyes wide. "You lied to me. You told me Adam was out of town when you knew all the time that he was right here in his cabin."

"No, I did go out of town," Adam said, trying to mitigate the damage. "Just not that evening. It had already started to snow, and I didn't want Miss Flynn to freeze standing on the station when your husband had forgotten all about her."

That pleased Marian and turned her mood around. After all, that meant I was so unimportant to Jason that he'd forgotten to pick me up, and Adam had just been doing a favor to Jason and to me. But she hadn't let go of her grievance, not quite. She turned to me. "You let me talk about Adam as if you didn't know anything about him, when all the time you had a very good idea what he was like."

This time Adam turned to me. "So, what did my cousin say about me? Did it improve your impression of me, or am I a villain?"

"Ah…" Before I could think of a suitable answer, Hattie came in with a tray of hors d'oeuvres and set it down on a low table by the fire. Jason swung the bar cabinet open and asked what we all wanted to drink. In the midst of drinks, sausage balls, crab dip with toast and cheese straws, I was spared having to answer.

Adam scooped hot crab dip up with a toast triangle and popped it into his mouth, licking his fingers in enjoyment. "Hattie, I'll swear you're the best cook in Virginia. In all these years you've never cooked anything I didn't like. How much would I have to pay you to come cook for me?"

"Aw, Mr. Adam, you know I couldn't leave Miss Marian. You need to get yourself a wife—one that can cook."

Adam laughed. "Women who want to cook are getting scarce, and women who want to move to a modest house on an isolated plantation are even scarcer." He looked at me. "How about you, Miss Flynn? Would you want to come cook at my place?"

I laughed, fairly sure we were joking and glad to see that Marian was no longer brooding but enjoying the evening. "Oh, you don't want me. I can't cook."

He took a long sip of his drink, said, "That's smooth bourbon, Jason. You still finding bottles from Grandpa Marbury?"

"No, I bought it at the ABC store. We emptied the old man's wine cellar a good while ago," Jason said, shaking his head in regret.

Marian sat on the sofa closest to the fireplace, and I sat on the matching sofa opposite her. Jason brought his glass of bourbon to the piecrust table and sat beside his wife. That left Adam standing by the fireplace, his arm up on the mantel. "This fireplace really puts out a lot of heat," he said, and stepped over in front of me. "May I?"

"Sure."

He was a big man, but there was ample room for both of us. Still, he sat close, his thigh casually pressed against mine. I didn't meet his eyes, but instead looked at Marian and Jason. They were both elegantly dressed for dinner, Jason obviously having notice enough to don a Brooks Brothers suit with a creamy turtleneck pullover. Adam and I were more casual, as befitted the poor relation and the employee. He wore jeans over polished black boots that he stretched toward the fire, and a thick olive green cable knit sweater. I felt his arm, casually slung over the back of the sofa, lightly touching my shoulder.

We four sat snacking and sipping, our silence broken by the crackle of the fire. We seemed to have exhausted conversation topics after we'd covered the food and drink. Then Adam tried again: "Any damage from the snow and ice?"

"Not that we've discovered," Jason said. "Lucas said there are some trees down on the back side of the farm. He'll cut and stack them for firewood as soon as all the snow melts in the woods."

"I had a tree fall on one of the fences. Brought it down. I think I'll leave it down, so the deer can cut through and clean up the cornfield."

"Deer can jump fences, silly," Marian said.

"True, but I want to make it easy for the young ones. Since I'm not running cattle this year, I'm happy to let the deer or bears or any other creatures eat the last of the corn and soybeans. And I always plant a bird strip for the partridges."

For the first time, I felt a sense of affinity toward Adam. Whatever he thought about his cousin or Jason or me, a man who cared for animals couldn't be all bad. "That's a really nice thing to do," I said.

Marian said, "Kate, you remember I told you about how Adam—" but Jason cut her off.

"I've been too occupied with looking after Marian to do a lot of things on the farm I'd like to do," he said. "Now that Kate's here I plan to spend more time on the farm."

"As if you know what to do," Marian scoffed, obviously annoyed at having been interrupted. My stomach started to sink as I envisioned another night of barely-contained arguments.

To my relief, Nate appeared to say that dinner was ready. We trooped in and took our places. Marian and Jason sat at opposite ends of the table, while Adam and I faced each other across the middle. Hattie had taken the leaves out of the dining table, so it was cozier. In the center was a small silver bowl with a handful of half-opened daffodils and a few small branches of forsythia, flanked by candles in silver candlesticks. I was impressed all over again at how Hattie managed to get so much done. I hoped the Ashbys were paying her well.

"That centerpiece is lovely, Hattie," I said. "Where did the daffodils come from?"

"A sheltered spot near the garden shed," Hattie said. "Nate been watching them ever since the snow melted. The forsythia I cut a few days ago, the way I always did, so it can open inside."

"My mother used to love flowers," Marian said. "And so do I."

"They're especially welcome this time of year," I said, thinking longingly of spring and the chance to be outside again—maybe even without Marian.

We set to eating Hattie's delicious dinner. She had really outdone herself. We started with oyster soup, succulent oysters floating in a creamy, buttery broth. The main course was pot roast with gravy to put over the flaky hot rolls, glazed sweet potatoes and turnip greens. I'd never cared for them, mainly because I had only had them canned, but Hattie had cooked them with bits of ham and cubes of turnip, and they were delicious.

"Hattie, you remembered my favorite foods," Adam said.

She smiled with pride; it was obvious that Adam was one of her favorite people. "Right down to the dessert, Mr. Adam," she said. "It's three-layer caramel cake."

"You're the only person I know who makes that," he said. "I should have asked and saved room for dessert."

"You can take home what you don't eat," she said, without waiting for Marian to offer it.

"Do you still have that dog?" Jason asked, changing the subject away from Hattie's obvious affection for his rival. The pause he put before the last word of the question indicated that he wasn't fond of the animal in question, or perhaps all dogs.

"Shep? Yes. I'm sorry he muddied your pants."

"Oh, that was months ago," Marian said. "I'm sure Jason has forgotten all about it."

I wasn't so sure about that, but I was glad another tiff didn't break out because of it. Instead, I focused on the caramel cake. The layers were a rich, buttery yellow with brown sugar frosting that had been spread over them while the cake was warm, so it soaked in. The outer frosting was thick and sugary, like eating pralines.

Adam left soon afterward, thanking Marian and Jason for inviting them. He took my hand and leaned in close to say, "I can't believe you lasted this long, but I still think you need to be careful." I don't know if Marian or Jason heard, but I pretended he'd said something else, and returned, "It's been a pleasure seeing you again too," perhaps a little more perkily than was necessary.

He gave me a quizzical look, nodded, and left.

Chapter 7

The next morning Marian greeted me with a big smile and urged me to look outside. "It's like Adam brought springtime with him," she said. "You liked him, didn't you? Better than Jason?"

I didn't know how to answer that. It seemed that no matter which choice I made, I might be in trouble. "I liked him a lot," I said. "And he obviously cares for you."

That seemed to satisfy her. "Look outside, Kate. It's glorious!" she said, in one of her typical mercurial changes of topic.

In fairness, though, it *was* glorious outside. The landscape seemed to have changed overnight. Maple branches were fuzzy red against a brilliant blue sky, and new grass had sprung up where snow had so recently covered everything. As a city girl, I hadn't paid much attention to the weather, merely checking to see if I needed a coat or umbrella, but at Marbury Hill weather was an ever-present element.

"We must go riding today," she proclaimed. "You can persuade Jason to let us."

I wasn't sure about that, but when I asked, he made no objection. "I was half hoping you'd say no," I confessed. "I'm not a good rider and I don't have suitable clothes."

"Oh, what you've got on is just fine. We don't ride to the hunt or anything like that, so we don't have special clothing for riding."

"I can hardly stay on a horse; it's not a pretty sight."

He laughed. "I'm not much better. Marian will love it that she does something better than we do. Let's give her a morning's enjoyment, shall we?"

As we three started down the lane toward the stable, Marian suddenly broke into a run. Jason ran after her and when he caught up, she threw her arms around him and said, "Jason, promise me you won't kill me today when the world is so beautiful. If you must do it, wait for some dark ugly night." Then, as if she had said nothing out of the ordinary, she fell into step between us. I shot a look of alarmed confusion at Jason; he responded with a shrug of his eyebrows.

The stable was as I remembered it: cool and dark, with a rectangle of light coming from the open door, and smaller rectangles from behind each of the stalls. The air was pungent with the fragrance of hay mixed with sweat and manure. The horses whinnied a welcome. They'd been cooped up during the snow just as we had.

Marian strode to Jeff's stall and put her hands through the wooden bars toward her big red horse. For a moment he moved away, eyes dilated and nostrils flaring. "Jeff? What's wrong? There's something wrong with him, Jason!" she cried. "Have you done something to him?"

"Of course not."

"Jeff, don't you remember me?" she asked. "It's all right."

I held my breath and hoped that her beloved horse would show her more affection than most humans had. He shifted from one foot to another. Then he bounded toward her, nickering a high sound of greeting. He pushed his head against the bars so Marian could caress him. She laid her head against his, tears rolling down her face. "Jeff, you do still love me," she crooned. "We're going riding!"

Jason pushed open the harness room door and looked around for Lucas before reluctantly taking down the saddles.

"Let me do that!" Marian commanded. "You don't know the first thing about how to treat horses." She led Jeff out of his stall and threw the saddle over his back. As I watched, fascinated, she tightened the belly band, got the reins around his neck and the bit into his mouth. She held out the reins to me. "Here, hold him while I saddle the other two. Jason will never get it done."

Lucas appeared and took over saddling the other two. Marian held Jeff, caressing his ears and nose. "Your horse is Champion," she told me. "Jason's is Bess. Bess is old and gentle, just right for Jason to ride."

"I should take Bess," I said. "I don't ride very well."

"I'm sure you ride better than Jason does," she countered. "You'd better let him have Bess."

Jason's face reddened but he looked away and said nothing. In that instant Marian leaped into the saddle, dug her heels into Jeff's side and cantered away. I stared, dumfounded and impressed at her grace and skill as a rider. I was watching her instead of the course ahead of her, and missed seeing the danger she was hurtling toward.

Jason saw. He snatched Champion's reins away from me, leaped onto the mount and raced after Marian. He came abreast of her and grabbed Jeff's reins just before she reached the gate. Jeff reared awkwardly and almost threw Marian, but she managed to stay on and turned angrily on Jason: "Why did you stop me?!"

"Jeff can't take hurdles and gates anymore; he's too old for that! You need to take it slow with him for his own good. If you can't keep him to a walk, we might have to have him put down."

Marian's face rippled with anger. "Killing comes easy to you, doesn't it?" she charged. "I stood by and watched you kill once, but I won't again. You leave Jeff alone or you'll be sorry."

Jason jerked Jeff's reins and brought the horse around. The muscles in both Jason and Marian's faces twitched, as if both were barely controlling their anger. Jason took a deep breath said in a steely calm voice, "Be more careful, Marian. Jeff can't do the tricks anymore that you trained him to do. You could have killed him, and yourself as well."

"You'd like that, wouldn't you? It would fit right in with your plans."

"No," he said wearily and impatiently. He slid down from Champion and went to open the gate and wait while we rode through—me barely sticking on Bess, Marian holding Jeff to a walk as requested.

"Go ahead. I'll catch up," he told us, leading Champion through and closing the gate behind us. Marian rode on ahead, her jaw set with annoyance. I looked back toward the gate and felt a chill despite the warm day at the way Jason was staring at Marian's back.

A few minutes later he rode up beside us with an even smile and said, "You know, it really is a lovely day for a ride, Marian. I'm glad you suggested it."

Looks like Marian isn't the only one capable of sudden mood swings, I thought.

He reached across to pat Marian's hand where it held the reins. "I'm just worried about you, honey. Accidents can happen in a split second, before you're aware of danger."

None of us spoke further as we rode down the bridle trail until the river came into view, and across it, a thin trail of smoke coming up from the woods. "That's Adam's house," Marian said to me, pointing. "He has land on both sides of the river, but his house is on the other side." When I didn't say anything, she went on, "He'll probably invite us over sometime soon."

"I don't know why you think that," Jason said. "He's never invited us but once."

"He likes Kate," Marian announced, in a tone that allowed no disagreement.

She turned Jeff around and headed back to the house.

After lunch Jason went into the library to catch the news and I went upstairs with Marian. "Do you want me to read to you?"

"No," she said. "I think I'll take a nap."

"Then you won't mind if I go walking?"

"You didn't like riding?"

"I feel safer on the ground."

"I'd rather ride than anything else in the world," she sighed. "If I knew I'd never ride again, I think I'd want to die." She gripped my arm. "You heard Jason threaten to kill Jeff. Promise me you won't let him do that."

I wasn't sure I could let or not let the man who signed my paycheck do anything, but Marian seemed to need comfort. "I don't think he meant it," I said with more confidence than I felt. "He was just embarrassed and angry. But I will speak to him."

"Right now?"

"Maybe when he's in a better mood."

She nodded, but I could tell my answer didn't satisfy her—any more than it did me. I pulled on Marian's mother's boots, tied a scarf over my hair and found my gloves, then headed downstairs.

When I poked my head into the library and told Jason I was going walking, he said, "That's a good idea. I'll come along."

"Actually, I want to be alone," I said, my voice a little sharper than I intended. I was certain any conversation Jason would want to have with me would be about Marian, and I'd had enough of both of them for the day.

"Suit yourself." He shrugged and turned back to the TV.

I didn't deliberately plan to go to Adam's farm, but perhaps I subconsciously wanted to see him, to talk to someone who wasn't Jason or Marian. I followed the same trail we'd ridden this morning, but when I reached the point where we'd stopped and Marian had indicated Adam's cabin, I went on, down toward the river. The land sloped sharply, and I plunged downward, across open low grounds where birds picked at scattered seeds or dug for grubs. They flew up at my approach, then landed again and went about their food search.

Mud sucked at my shoes as I moved along parallel to the river until I found an opening through the undergrowth. I came out onto a small sandy beach where wild violets grew and a large flat rock overhung the water.

The river was swift in midstream, but closer to the bank it scarcely moved. I leaned out over the rock's edge and saw my shimmering reflection mirrored there: pale face framed by dark hair poking out from the red scarf, bright against the gray parka. I pulled off a glove and stirred the water with my fingertip. It was icy cold. When it cleared, I saw another face reflected beside mine: Adam's. Startled, I leaped up so quickly that I almost lost my balance. He caught me with strong, steady arms.

"So, Miss Flynn, you came to visit me. Excellent!" He was wearing the same jeans from the night before, boots and a shaggy plaid jacket. He relaxed his grip on me from the strength of catching my fall to a more gentle hold. I pulled away from him, but not very far.

"I didn't mean to invade your property," I said, embarrassed from both being caught and almost falling.

"No harm done. I won't prosecute you for trespassing. According to the law I'm entitled to whatever driftwood and animals show up on my property, and that might include you."

My heart started to pound as I realized I was actually trespassing and he might well be angry. Then he cracked up and I realized he was joking.

"I was walking Shep when I saw you and decided to join you," he said. "I didn't mean to startle you, especially not that much." He grinned, and then whistled. A large dark Lab trotted toward us, tail wagging. He reached down and patted the dog's head. Shep dropped to his belly beside his owner. "Shep saw you first, but then he noticed a covey of partridges, and pointed them."

"He hunts?"

"He does. I don't. I turned toward you, but he stayed to flush the birds. Such a diligent hunter," he said approvingly, ruffling the fur on Shep's head. "So did they let you out for the afternoon? Or are you running away?"

"Both. I needed to get out of the house."

He guided me to sit back down on the warm flat rock and sat close beside me. "I didn't have the opportunity to talk to you last night, so I'm happy you showed up, and practically on my doorstep! I'm not sure who was more determined to keep us from talking alone, Marian or Jason, but it was obvious. So now that you've spent time at Marbury Hill, do you think my statements were accurate?"

"You mean about Marian being crazy? I don't know. She's referred to the idea of Jason killing her at least half a dozen times since I got here, but I can't tell if she says it just to get a rise out of him or because she's… " I trailed off.

"Actually afraid he might kill her?" Adam finished for me.

"Maybe," I shrugged. "Or afraid that he might leave her or hurt her in some other way. Half the time, she's angry at him, scared of him or both; the other half she's desperately trying to win his approval. It's honestly rather exhausting."

"Love can make people do strange things," he said.

"Of course, so can the end of love. Maybe that's what she's scared of."

"You sound as if you're speaking from experience. What strange thing did love—or the end of it—lead you to do?"

"Take this job," I said more lightheartedly than I felt.

"Why did you take the job? I've wondered ever since that first day. Supposedly, the place is cursed. And perhaps that's true: it's already cast its spell on you, or you'd have left before now." He paused. "Or maybe it's Jason? Has he charmed you the way he charmed Marian?"

"What? No! I just needed a job, and this one pays much better than the others I was qualified for." I was irritated by his assumption, so I asked somewhat challengingly, "What about you? Has love led you to do something strange?"

"Not especially, but then most people would think I'm a strange bird to begin with, living in an overseer's cabin with my aged dog, letting a thousand acres of land lie fallow and unproductive."

I didn't dispute the point. "Have you ever been married?"

He shook his head. "From what I seen, marriage is a gamble and I'd probably lose. Marian's mother married for money, and you see how that turned out. My mother married for love and got the second-best land." He gestured to himself. "You see how that turned out."

"Eh, it could've gone worse," I said, gently teasing him. "Marian thinks you're great."

"Yes, but in terms of marriage material, I find it's best to look beyond one's cousins," he said with a grin. He'd been idly dragging a small stick back and forth in the water. Now he turned to face me, studying me with gray eyes that were so much like Marian's. "Last night she was angry that you'd let her talk without revealing that you knew me. What did she say about me?"

"What, you want more compliments? She said you were her shining knight, and that you were dashing and handsome."

He threw back his head and laughed, the sound echoing slightly off the water. "You'd already seen me. Didn't that tip you off that she might be crazy?"

"Oh, stop that," I protested. "To her you're handsome because you've been kind to her. That matters a lot more than how someone looks on the outside."

"Poor Marian," he said with a sad smile. "I feel sorry for her. Money can buy you a husband, but not a faithful one, or love and respect. Or safety."

I briefly debated asking him about one of Marian's wilder accusations and decided to take the plunge; perhaps he'd know more about it. "You know… she claims she saw Jason kill another woman," I said as casually as possible.

From the startled expression on his face I could tell that this was the first time he had heard it. "*What?*" He shook his head in confusion. "Do you think it could be one of those things she says to get a rise out of him?"

"I'm not sure. I don't think so, because she only told it to me. It sounds bizarre, but what if it's true?"

"Then she's not safe there, and should call the police," he stated.

"Do you think Jason could have actually killed someone?" I asked, realizing that I didn't actually know him that well and couldn't say for absolutely certain that he wouldn't have done anything so horrible.

"I don't know," Adam said, shaking his head. "I think anyone could probably kill if driven to it, but I'm not sure Jason would put in that kind of effort."

"So you're saying he's not too ethical to kill, he's just too lazy?" I said with a smile.

"Something like that," Adam agreed, laughing a bit.

As much as I enjoyed sharing a joke with him, I couldn't quite let go of the possibility that Marian might be telling the truth. "If she did call the police about witnessing a murder, would they believe her? Jason told me she tried to slit her wrists once, and when she told the police that he had tried to kill her, they didn't take her seriously."

"She's at a disadvantage in this town," he conceded. "Our great aunt was institutionalized for insanity and just about everyone here knows about it, though nobody would say anything about it to Marian's face. It was probably bipolar disorder or extreme anxiety, something that now could be treated with medications."

"Has Marian been treated for anything, or even diagnosed?"

"Not to my knowledge, but some people like to keep their … issues secret."

I sighed. "You know, I went on this walk to get away from Marian and Jason, and yet that's about all we've talked about."

"What would you like to talk about? Mention a topic and I'll have a go at it!"

"Thanks, but I think I'd better go. Technically, I'm still on the clock." I stood and brushed grit and debris from the back of the parka where I'd been sitting on the rock.

He stood up too. "Oh, don't go. You can't imagine how good it is to talk with you—even about my insane cousin and her potentially murderous husband. You're sane, and probably not too murderous." He gently touched the side of my face with the back of his hand. "And beautiful."

Just as I realized what was about to happen, he kissed me, softly at first then deeper as I responded to him, parting my lips and bringing my hand up to caress his wind-tanned cheek. Was this why I had left the house and headed in this direction? I asked myself. Was I hoping that something like this might happen? *Yes*, I admitted.

Before I was ready for the kiss to end, he lifted his head to look at me, but stayed so close I could feel his breath warm on my face. He loosened his hold on me, dropping his hands to clasp the small of my back. "I can see why Jason chose you."

I was thoroughly confused. "What do you mean?" What did Jason have to do with that kiss?

"Well, I mean, look at you," he said, his hands gesturing to my face and body. "I know he does; I saw the way he was eyeing you last night. But I bet Jason can't kiss like that."

"I wouldn't know," I said sternly. "And why are we even talking about him? For God's sake, can't anyone on this entire estate talk about something other than Jason or Marian?!" I pulled free of him and tried to walk off, even as the briars and mud hindered my progress.

"I'm sorry. Look, I'll drive you back to Marbury Hill," he offered.

"Thanks, but I'll walk. The conversation will be better, with no mention of a single Ashby!" I found the opening from the riverbank to the low grounds and pushed my way through, scratching my face on the thorny branch of a wild plum tree in the process.

"Come back and see me sometime?" he called after me. "I'll be thinking about you."

As I struggled through the muddy field and up the hill toward the bridle path, I began to doubt whether I was making the point I had intended to make, but it was too late. I wished I had taken him up on his offer of a drive; that way I could have kissed him once more in the car.

Chapter 8

I'd planned to slip quietly into my room, clean my boots and get some antiseptic on the scratches on my face, but Marian must have heard me come in. "Kate, Adam just called. He said he found some gloves down by the river. I told him you'd been walking down that way. Did you lose yours?"

I stuck my bare hands in the parka pocket and pulled out the red scarf, but no gloves. "I must have dropped them," I said, then remembered well enough taking them off when I sat down on the rock. When Adam kissed me, the gloves were the last thing on my mind.

"He said they must be yours, since he didn't think anybody else had walked there. He's going to bring them over."

"When?"

"In time for supper. He said it was lucky finding your gloves, since it would give him a good excuse to have another of Hattie's dinners. She's delighted, of course. She's always thought the sun rose and set in her 'Mr. Adam.' I used to be jealous that she liked him so much, but now I don't mind. Actually, I can understand it. He compliments her and I tend to take her for granted."

I had never been so exasperated with Marian than I was in that moment. *Wow,* I thought, *how big of you not to be jealous that someone else was being nice to your cousin; how insightful to see that it was because the cousin showed them kindness that you don't; and how thoughtful to fail to realize that perhaps you should be nicer to them too.* I was starting to feel as if the whole world revolved around Marian Ashby and her husband (who might or might not have nefarious plans for her), and the rest of us were expected to be grateful simply to share their orbit.

As I turned away, she said, "I think he likes you, Kate."

"You have a good cousin, Marian. I'm glad he comes here to look after you."

"Do you like him?" she persisted.

"Yes," I admitted.

"Better than you like Jason?"

I detected a bit of jealousy as usual, so I was glad I could answer her honestly,

"Much better than Jason."

That seemed to satisfy her. She glanced down at the boots I was wearing, her mother's boots. "The boots and parka suit you, Kate. Keep them if you want them."

"Thank you. I'll wear them as long as I'm here." Then, thinking how that might sound, I added, "As soon as I clean them I'll come in and read to you."

I cleaned and put away the boots, hung up the parka, brushed the twigs from my hair and washed my face, which thankfully showed almost no trace of my encounter with the wild plum tree. Then for most of the afternoon I read to Marian without remembering a thing I'd read. My mind was on Adam, and to a lesser extent on Jason. What was going on with those two? The enmity between them had been obvious in their voices when they spoke to each other, and Jason hated to hear Marian praise Adam. Did Marian want me to like Adam because she thought Jason might be interested in me? Or did she want to try to make Jason jealous? And how sad and lonely would someone have to be to try to use their cousin as a pawn in a game of egos?

I took a leisurely soak in the big claw-footed tub and then had to rush to get dressed. I chose a red wool dress that I'd worn on one of the other nights when the Ashbys dressed for dinner. When I dropped it over my shoulders it settled smoothly about my hips and moved easily as I walked toward the mirror. I wasn't sure how I'd behave around Adam, Marian or Jason tonight, but I figured I'd look damn good doing it. My momentary boost of confidence deflated as I realized that if both Marian and Adam thought Jason was paying special attention to me, this could be one of the most awkward, painful evenings ever. And at Marbury Hill, that was really saying something.

I went down early, wanting to be seated serenely in the library, reading a magazine or sipping some drink that would soothe my nerves. But as I came down the curving staircase, I saw Adam in the hall below, looking up at me.

Marian was holding his arm, guiding him not back to the library but into a room I hadn't entered before, the front parlor. "Kate, Adam's come over early. He couldn't wait to see you again."

He looked as awkward as I felt over Marian's less-than-subtle attempt at matchmaking. There was nothing polite either of us could say to that. I smiled and walked over to him, hoping we could put the afternoon's weirdness behind us. He had dressed up this evening too—no longer in jeans, but wearing a navy blazer and gray slacks, a shirt and perfectly knotted tie.

"Please excuse me for a moment," Marian said. "I'll leave you alone while I go speak to Hattie and find Jason." I could have sworn I heard her giggle as she left the room.

Adam laughed bashfully, then looked at me and took my hand. "Ordinarily I'd object to being 'fixed up,' but not after this afternoon."

"Yeah, I'm sorry I took off like that. I was just so tired of talking about—"

"No, you were right. Maybe a little overdramatic, but right. We were having a really great moment there, and I had to kill the mood by talking about them," he nodded over toward the rest of the house to indicate its main occupants.

"She doesn't know I saw you today," I said, remembering what had indeed been a great moment. He still held my hand and I didn't take it away.

"And I don't think she needs to know, either. I don't know how many women she thinks might walk on my property, but I was glad to use the gloves as an excuse to see you again." He dropped my hand and reached into his pocket. "Speaking of gloves." He handed them to me and I placed them on a table behind the sofa.

"You look really lovely tonight, Kate," he said, leaning close to my ear. A lock of his hair fell forward, touching my neck. I longed to push back the hair and kiss him, but I restrained myself. Then he murmured, "Quite a change from the hiking duds."

"You look lovely too," I said. "Very smartly dressed. Quite civilized."

"That was my intention. I wanted to show you that I can clean up pretty good."

I laughed, and he led me to the sofa by the fire. Glasses of wine had already been poured and stood on the coffee table beside a bowl of salted nuts. Adam handed me a glass of white wine and picked up a glass of red for himself.

"Should we wait for …?" I made the same nodding gesture he had made earlier to indicate Marian and Jason.

"Probably," he said glumly, then winked at me. "Screw it!" he said, downing a gulp of wine. "Say, when do you think you might come to my cabin for dinner?"

"What makes you think I'll do that?" I wondered if the thought about my coming to his cabin had been prompted by saying "screw."

"Because you're curious to see how I live," he said, and I had to admit he was right. "You want to know how the rustic noble sort-of-savage spends his days and nights."

"I'll probably wait a few days so you'll start missing me." I was flirting with him at the same time I was telling the truth. It had been a long time since I'd bantered with an attractive man.

"I'll start missing you as soon as I leave tonight."

"It's a good thing I know you're teasing, or I might actually fall for that line."

"What makes you think I'm teasing?"

"The look in your eyes and the way you smile."

"How do you know this isn't my most serious look?"

And just then, Marian returned, with Jason following.

Dinner was interminable. Hattie had as usual produced a marvelous meal, but I kept thinking about my conversation with Adam by the river, how well I actually knew Jason, how much I could trust anything Marian said and the way Jason had looked at Marian on the ride.

She praised Adam until I wanted to slip under the table, but he kept a sardonic, half-amused expression as he ate and sipped wine. He praised the food, inquired after Jason's farming operations and recalled a few amusing incidents from Marian's childhood that delighted her. Whenever I met his gaze across the table I could almost feel his lips on mine, and the thought made me smile.

Then I started thinking about how close he and Marian were, and wondered if playing with other people's emotions was something just Marian did, or if it were a family tradition. *Marian could be telling the truth*, I thought, *or she could just be playing Jason—and me. Adam seemed to enjoy playing Jason as well. Could he possibly be playing me too?* I wondered.

Jason seemed well aware of Adam's strategy, based on the occasional flashes of irritation I saw in his eyes as he answered Adam's questions about farming. I thought I might have seen something else too: a flash of jealousy. But was it toward Adam for his attention to Marian, or for his attention to me? And why did I almost like the idea that Jason might be a bit jealous because of me? Was I falling under some kind of spell, or even the curse of Marbury Hill?

We had scarcely finished Hattie's pecan pie and coffee with Adam pushed his plate away and rising, held out his hand to Jason and announced, "This has been pleasant, but I'm off for home. I'm going to Richmond early in the morning."

"When will you be back?" Marian asked. "You know how much I enjoy having you visit, and just knowing that you're close by."

Me too, I thought with a slight thrill, but wouldn't allow myself to say it aloud or even to meet Adam's gaze.

"Hard to say. Business calls. I'll come by the next time I'm at the farm. I prom- ise." He spoke to Marian and squeezed her hand, but I felt his words were for me as well.

The door had hardly closed when Marian turned to me and said, "Isn't he wonderful? And he's really gone on you."

"Ah yes, the perfect Adam," Jason scoffed. "It's such a shame you couldn't mar- ry him, Marian, rather than having to make do with me. But perhaps you can get some vicarious thrills through Kate by setting them up."

I felt stung by his remark, but also sympathetic for the hurt in his voice.

"Oh, grow up, Jason," Marian snapped.

Jason headed toward the library, Marian headed upstairs and I headed back to the parlor to see if there was any wine left.

Days passed, of clouds and spring rain. We read more books, altered more clothing and played more cards, unable to work outside or take long walks. I began to miss Adam, wondering where he was and when he might be back. I still had his phone number, but I forced myself not to call him. He was the one who had left; he should be the one to call and invite me over, as he'd said.

Finally came a day that was sunny, and Marian suggested that we dig the flow- erbeds and paint the lawn furniture, an activity I wouldn't have thought of. "We'll have to ask Jason," she said. "It's my house and my money, but I always have to ask him. One of these days I'm going to do something without asking him."

To my surprise, Jason agreed, and sent Lucas into town for paint. Lucas or Nate could dig the flowerbeds, he said, and we could paint furniture and shutters.

We got started right after lunch. Lucas had taken down the shutters and laid them across saw horses, and had spread a tarp on the grass and arranged the lawn chairs atop it.

Marian was a little awkward at first, dipping the brush without scraping it across the paint can, so that she left a trail of paint drips. I started to correct her, but I figured it was her home and her paint, and she was entitled to do as she pleased. I let her see me slide the brush correctly, and she soon caught on.

After a while she stepped back to admire her handiwork. "Up close it looks awful, streaky instead of smooth," she said ruefully, "but from my window it will look fine."

"You don't have to just look at it from your window," I objected. "You can come down here and we'll all sit on a lovely morning and have breakfast, or drinks in the afternoon."

"That sounds nice," she said, and went back to painting. "Maybe."

After a while she asked, "Did I ever tell you about my great aunt?"

"What about her?" I didn't say that both Jason and Adam had mentioned her. I wanted to hear Marian's story and perspective.

"Her name was Varina, and she was in love with somebody her parents didn't want her to marry. She would slip out to meet him. Then her father found out and locked her in her room. She told him she was going to have a baby. I don't know if it was true or not, but her father said he'd keep her locked in until it was born and then take the baby away where she'd never see it. Varina screamed and cried and said she'd kill him or kill herself, but nothing she said did any good. They locked her in her room and she refused to eat. Nobody would give in. Then one morning early they heard a scream, and they found her lying right there, dead."

I stared at Marian as the dipped the brush into the paint bucket and drew a large cross on the flagstones. "X marks the spot where Aunt Varina died," she said calmly. "There were some sheets tied together hanging out of her window, up there—my window now. Nobody knew for sure if she was planning to meet her lover and run away, because she was dead and they couldn't ask her." She pointed up, still holding the dripping paintbrush in her hand, and in my mind I could see knotted white sheets moving gently in a morning breeze, throwing shadows against the wall. I shivered, trying to dispel the image. I closed my eyes tightly, then opened them and the image was gone. The shadows were made by sunlight coming through an overhanging branch.

Marian went on, "A strange man came to her funeral, but as soon as it was over he disappeared and never came back."

I'd stopped my painting to listen to the story, saddened and horrified. Marian went back to work painting a chair, her hand steady and the paint going on as smoothly as if she had said something bland or amusing. She continued, "Varina's mother and father said they were to blame, which they were—and they were very sorry, but it was too late then to feel sorry. That's what happens when people lock someone up like an animal and don't love them. Jason will be sorry someday, won't he?"

I didn't answer. I couldn't.

"Kate, don't you think that's a sad story?"

"Oh yes, absolutely, but I'm confused. I thought your aunt died in a mental hospital." As soon as I said it, I wished I hadn't, but Marian didn't seem bothered by my knowledge of that aunt.

"Did Jason tell you that? That was another Varina. There's more than one in my family."

I wasn't so sure. Had Marian imagined this Varina's death, just as she imagined being rescued by a handsome knight?

"Tell me about your family, Kate. You never talk about them, and I talk a lot about my family. Is everybody in your family dead?"

"No, only my mother."

"Are you an only child like me?"

"No. My sister and her husband live in California."

"She never calls or writes you. Does she know you're here?"

I hesitated. If no one knew I was at Marbury Hill, was I in danger? "I did write her. I gave the letter to Jason to mail."

Our eyes met for a moment. "You could call her," Marian suggested. I nodded.

"What about your father? Doesn't he care about you?"

I didn't want to go into my resentment at how he'd neglected my mother. "He's remarried and lives in Florida. I don't get on very well with his new wife. She's just a few years older than I am."

"You're lucky to have a father and sister, even if they are a long ways away. At least they're alive, and you could call them if you need them. I don't have anybody but Adam, and he's away a lot. I wish I had brothers and sisters. My mother had a baby before me and one afterward, but they were both born dead. When my parents saw how ugly I was, they may have been glad they didn't have any others."

"Oh, Marian, you shouldn't say things like that!" I cringed at the pain she must have felt to think that.

"Why not? It's true. One night when they thought I was asleep, I heard them arguing. My father was trying to persuade my mother to have more children. But she said, 'Look at Marian. I don't know why you want to perpetuate such traits at the cost of my health.' "

"Are you completely sure she said that? No offense, but that doesn't sound like the kind of thing a child would understand."

"I was seven then and very wide awake. I'd crept downstairs for something to eat. I wasn't supposed to do that. My mother tried to keep me from overeating, but Hattie would leave snacks where she was sure I could find them. Anyway, I was tiptoeing quietly and they didn't hear me. I had to look up 'perpetuate' in the dictionary, but even before I read what it meant, I knew that my mother didn't like my looks. I took after my father, so I wasn't ever going to be beautiful and graceful like her. When I saw the definition, I burst into tears and ran to the mirror to look at myself. I decided I had to marry a handsome man, so maybe our children would look like him instead of me, but handsome men want to marry beautiful women. I think Jason is handsome, but he doesn't want us to have children."

What evil people can do with a few words, I thought, and wished that Marian's mother had lived to see the havoc her attitude had created in her unloved daughter. Or if she'd seen it and somehow made amends. But how could apologizing change what couldn't be taken back? Jason couldn't undo the rejection of the past, no matter how loving he was or how much he did for Marian, and I felt sympathy for him even trying to do that, though I wondered how much his heart was in it.

I envisioned Marian with a plain husband who told her how lucky he was to have married her and several children who thought she was beautiful because they loved her and because she was their mother. What could her life have been like with more confidence and faith in herself and her worth?

However, Marian had sought out a distinctly non-plain man, and had even married him. She wanted a handsome man, a hero, who would make other women envy her and she had hoped their envy and his attention would make her feel beautiful. But her relentless focus on looks had only made her more miserable. My mother used to say, 'Be careful what you wish for, because that's probably what you'll get.' Marian had wanted a handsome husband, and she'd gotten Jason. Had he made her feel beautiful and loved, even for a moment? If I could be sure that he had, I could forgive him for almost anything.

We finished painting the first coat, cleaned up the brushes and tamped down the lids on the paint can before we put it all away. As we turned to one of the flowerbeds, the sunlight was warm on my back and the earth beneath my fingers was soft and damp. As I broke crumbled lumps of manure into the flowerbeds, I tried to pretend that the moisture on my face was perspiration, but I knew better. It was tears for Marian, the imprisoned princess.

I was just falling asleep that night when Jason tapped on my door. "Kate, can you take this to Marian while I go back down and clean the kitchen. Hattie dislikes me enough already, without holding it against me for messing up her kitchen."

As he handed me the plate with a cup of warm milk on it, some of the milk slopped over the edge. He whipped out a handkerchief and wiped the lip of the cup clean.

Two little yellow pills lay beside the cup. "What are those?" I asked.

"A sedative. If she doesn't take them, bring them back downstairs to me. I don't want her saving them up for a possible suicide attempt."

"Are they that powerful?"

"Not singly, but enough of almost any medication can kill."

When I knocked on Marian's door and said, "It's Kate," she called out, "It's unlocked." At the sight of the cup, she demanded, "Is that some concoction Jason's fixed for me? What is it? Is it poison?"

"I think it's just warm milk. He wants you to drink it along with these pills."

"You drink some. Show me it's not poison," she demanded.

"You're not worried I might have germs?"

"Not half as worried as I am about being poisoned."

I sipped the milk. It tasted a bit strange, but I didn't have much to compare it with. I don't like warm milk, so it wouldn't have tasted good to me no matter how pure it was.

Reassured, she took the cup, drank the entire contents and handed it back. "I don't want the pills. Flush them down the toilet."

"Jason said you need a sedative."

"All right. I'll take one, just one. Then will you and Jason be satisfied?"

I didn't like being teamed with Jason in urging her to take pills, especially as I didn't know what the pills contained. She took one off the plate and swallowed it without any liquid.

When I gave Jason the leftover pill, he thanked me and dropped it into a half filled bottle he kept in his desk, and motioned toward the fireplace. "Sit down and have a drink with me. Please." He held out a goblet into which he'd already poured a drink, cupping the bowl in his hand like someone making an offering to a goddess.

It was brandy, warm and golden like the fire. *Like Jason's eyes*, I thought, aware that those eyes were watching me. Neither of us spoke. I could hear the hissing of the fire, a limb brushing against the window, the grandfather clock ticking and the beat of my heart.

There were a lot of questions I wanted to ask him, but I didn't dare. Had he done everything he could to make Marian feel beautiful, safe and loved? What if he'd told me that the pills were actually poison? What if he admitted he'd killed someone, as Marian had told me? I didn't think her accusations were true, but if they were, she could be in real danger—as could I.

We sipped our brandy in silence. When my glass was empty, Jason took it from me and set it next to his on the table, then reached for my hands and pulled me against him, so close I could no longer see the dark pointed brows or black hair, only the golden animal eyes. I realized how easy it would be to kiss him, to close the library door and indulge every bit of loneliness, desire and curiosity I'd felt since I got here, and it scared me. I pulled back and left the room, calling "Good night" hastily over my shoulder.

When I opened my door the next morning expecting to see Hattie or Nate with a tray of coffee, Jason stood holding it instead. "Kate, I apologize for my behavior last night. I promise that it won't happen again, and I hope I didn't go too far and that you'll stay with us." He emphasized the last word as if to remind himself (and possibly me) that Marian was my primary focus here.

"I accept your apology," I said. "But I'm still planning to leave as soon as I can arrange it. I still have the return portion of my ticket." I didn't tell him what I feared: that it might be I and not he who instigated another encounter.

"Oh, you can't leave now. We need you more than ever, especially Marian. She almost died last night."

"What happened?!" My mind raced with possibilities, and with shame that while she was in danger I'd been drinking brandy with her husband. What kind of person had I become?

"I don't know. You only gave her the one pill, right?"

"Yes, I brought the other back to you. She didn't even want to take one."

"Hattie may have slipped her some homemade concoction of something. She's always telling Marian about old folk remedies. Or Marian may have started hoarding the sedatives before I began keeping count of them. Or it may not even be deliberate. She could have had a reaction to something she ate or drank during the day. At any rate, we almost lost her."

"Did you get a doctor?"

He shook his head. "No doctor would make a house call out here, especially at night. If I'd called the Rescue Squad, they'd have just told me to take Marian's pulse every two minutes, give her liquid if she seemed dehydrated, give her a couple of aspirin then bring her in to the hospital in the morning. We've gone through that before. Fortunately, she seems all right this morning. Will you go see her as soon as you've finished breakfast?"

"Of course."

When I went into her room, Marian lay sprawled across her bed in a tangle of pink satin sheets, her mouth gaped open in a snore. I bent to smooth the covers and position her head better on the pillow. She didn't stir as I lifted her head and shifted the pillow. My fingers touched a tiny round object: one of the yellow pills.

Had I dropped it off the plate when I brought her the milk? I remembered there being only two pills on the plate and I'd seen her take one. I knew that I'd returned the other to Jason. Where had this one come from? Had someone brought her pills during the night? Had she actually been saving them, as Jason suggested? If she'd intended to take enough to kill herself, how had this one escaped her attention?

I slipped the pill into my pocket, intending to put it in the bottle and check the label the first chance I got. If Marian didn't pull through, I'd be the one to blame. My fingerprints would be on the cup as I'd picked it up and drunk at her request. It occurred to me that when Jason wiped up the spilled milk from the cup, he had also probably wiped his fingerprints off.

Marian stirred and opened her eyes, then sat up, stretching and pushing back the tangle of sheets. "What time is it, Kate? I feel as if I'd slept for months, and I had nightmares the whole time, about taking little yellow pills that would kill me. Thank God that was only a dream."

Chapter 9

As usual, Marian's moods could switch from morose to excited within a few seconds. Two days after what Jason had called her "near death" night, she came knocking on my door before I was up, and before Hattie had brought coffee.

I'd awakened to the sweet sound of rain, which I'd always taken as a sign from nature that it was a day to sleep in.

"It's Marian," she called gaily, opening the door before I could get to it. "Hurry up, Kate. Hattie has breakfast ready downstairs and then we can open up the big parlor. You haven't seen that. We used the little parlor when Adam was here—what my mother used to call the Morning Room."

"But it's raining."

"That's why it's a perfect day to open up rooms and explore. We can't work outside, but we can take the covers off everything and get ready for a party."

"A party?" I rubbed my eyes and began to pull on clothes, hardly aware of what I was wearing. A party seemed like a concept from another planet.

"Yes. We can invite people over soon and have Hattie make cookies and little sandwiches and tea."

After breakfast Hattie went with us to the big parlor and helped us remove and fold furniture covers. The furniture was magnificent, beautifully grained wood that gleamed in elegant lines of Duncan Phyfe and Chippendale. My head reeled with the amount all that furniture would bring at an antique auction. Even without the house and land, the Ashbys were wealthy with this furniture alone. And it was hidden away at Marbury Hill, never used or even seen.

"Mummy used to sit there," Marian said, pointing to a red velvet wingback chair by the fireplace. "My father would sit on the sofa with me on his lap. Sometimes Adam and his parents and sister would be here too. Adam looks like my mother, don't you think?" She pointed to the huge formal portrait above the mantel that I'd been aware of from the moment we'd come in, but had avoided looking at. Even as paint on canvas, Marian's mother dominated the room. "That's the way I remember her," Marian said.

I studied the portrait. I'd become accustomed to Marian's appearance that she no longer seemed plain or dowdy to me—until I compared her to her mother. Marian was as washed out as her mother was vivid, and where her mother's hairline dipped to a point in the center of her forehead and swept back dramatically into a high crown of perfectly arranged ebony curls, Marian merely had a low forehead and undistinguished features. Only the eyes were the same, both sets gray and full of mystery. And Marian's were full of tears.

"Can you imagine what it was like to look like me and have a mother who looked like that?" she demanded, in a way that somehow seemed accusatory. "Mummy didn't take me many places. She was embarrassed to have such a plain child, as if she'd done something wrong. All the ruffled dresses and fancy hairdos just made me look silly. Most mothers would have put a child like me in jeans and sneakers and gotten them into Little League or something like that, but she wanted me to look just like she did when she was that age, even if there was no way I could."

I thought about how I'd been giving Marian a gradual makeover since I'd arrived, defining her eyebrows, styling her hair, shortening her hemlines. My reasons were different from her mother's, or so I told myself, but perhaps she heard the same message: that she wasn't good enough.

Abruptly, she turned from her mother's portrait to her father's, smaller and on a side wall. "I look more like him," she said, pointing. "We both have dishwater hair, short necks and square jaws. Daddy wanted a girl who looked like Mummy, especially after she died."

I didn't ask what had caused her mother's death. I was half afraid I'd hear another horror story of murder or suicide. I wanted to leave the room, throw myself back into bed and dream of happy families and joyful lives, but Marian kept talking, growing more and more agitated.

"Sometimes my father would come in here and stand looking at her portrait. He didn't know I was watching him. After a while he had the furniture covered and the parlor closed up. Each time he'd come and look at her portrait, he and I would go walking or riding and he'd be sad and quiet. When he'd look at me he was looking for my mother's face, and it wasn't there. I wanted to be beautiful for him, but I couldn't! I just kept on living, looking like *this!*" She grabbed a handful of her hair and tore at it, pulling out a fistful of strands.

I threw my arms around her to keep her from hurting herself. "Marian, Marian, stop it! Stop torturing yourself like this. Your appearance is nothing to be ashamed of!"

"I know how I look. I have a mirror."

"Marian, you look just fine. And besides, what makes you beautiful is what the people you love see in you."

She laughed bitterly. "None of that matters to Jason. He's never loved me. He married me because he was afraid I'd tell what I know, and now he wants to get rid of me." She clutched my sleeve. "Promise me when something happens to me you'll tell Adam everything I've said and give him my box."

Once again, we were back to Marian's favorite topic. The day's ruin was complete. "Why don't you just tell Adam all of this yourself?"

"Jason never leaves me alone with Adam, and he takes away my phone so I can only use it when I'm around him. Adam might not believe me anyway, but he would believe *you*."

"I don't know, he told me—" I stopped, realizing he couldn't have said anything at dinner about Marian's secret.

Marian was quick. "He told you what? And when? I thought there was something going on between you two when he brought back your gloves. I told Jason so, but he said I was wrong, just jumping to conclusions because I wanted him to like you and to come here often."

"I talked to him when I went walking and lost my gloves," I admitted.

"Well, if you've already talked with him about it, then there's no reason for me not to talk to him! We can both walk over to his farm," she said.

"As long as Jason doesn't want to tag along, we could totally do that," I said, eager to transfer the burden of Marian's secret completely over to Adam.

"You can think of something to say to make him leave us alone if you really want to help me." Suddenly, a shadow fell across her face and her eyes narrowed suspiciously. "But you don't, do you? Of course you won't; nobody will help me. If Jason kills me, it will be partly your fault. How will you feel, knowing you could have helped me escape and didn't?"

This was exhausting. "Marian, Jason's not going to kill you," I soothed her, as I'd been doing ever since I came to Marbury Hill."

"You say that because you're on *his* side."

"I'm not on anybody's side. If I can think of some way for you to visit Adam or call him, I will. Now, why don't we have a look at the next room?"

"No! Not that one, not ever!" she cried, backing away from me. She pointed accusingly at me and exclaimed, "I knew it!" before bolting out of the room.

I followed her out into the hallway and started up the steps. She turned to me and yelled, "Quit following me!"

"But I just want to make sure you're okay!"

"I don't want anything from you. I just want to be left alone. Do you understand?" Without waiting for an answer, she ran up to her room and slammed the door. I heard it lock.

I went back into the parlor and stared up at the portrait of Marian's mother, with its haunting likeness to Adam. I didn't hear Jason's footsteps, but the rich winey smell of his pipe tobacco signaled his approach. I didn't turn or move away from him, even when he put his arm around my shoulder. I stood very still, allowing myself to enjoy the feeling, until a guilty conscience made me pull away.

"Rejection noted and accepted, Kate," he sighed. "Where's Marian?"

"Upstairs. She said she wants to be alone. Do you think she'll do anything dangerous?"

"I don't know, and sometimes I don't care. I'm tired of trying to intervene in her activities. I want it to be over. I want to be a husband, not a warden."

Whether or not his words were intended as a reprimand for me, whose job it was to be her warden, the hurt at having failed must have shown in my face.

"I don't mean to put all the responsibility off on you. You've done a fine job and I thought you two were getting along well. What set her off today?"

"I'm not sure. We were talking about her parents and Adam, and I suggested taking a look at the next room." I definitely wasn't going to tell him she'd asked my help in escaping from him.

"Poor Marian," he said as I'd heard him say so many times. "It's no wonder she's the way she is. Just looking at that old girl's portrait shakes me up, and she wasn't even my mother." He studied the portrait, then looked away. "Could you come into the library for a bit? I have some actual secretarial work for you; it could be a nice break from dealing with Marian."

While I wrote checks for his signature and typed letters, he went over the farm accounts and then studied bulletins on farming. "I hate for the tenants to know more about my job here than I do," he said. "One of these days I'll be able to tell them when we should start planting, instead of asking them when. That is, if I'm here that long."

I glanced at him, but made no response. Both he and Marian made dramatic statements intended to stir my sympathy, and I was trying to let some of them pass without comment.

Hattie brought lunch into the library without being asked, and began to set two places on a card table.

"Ask Mrs. Ashby if she'd like to come down and have lunch with us," Jason said.

"I done already asked her. She say no."

"Is she all right?"

"As right as can be expected," she muttered, and went out.

"Perhaps I should go up and stay with her," I suggested. "She *was* upset when she left."

"She'll be all right. Otherwise Hattie wouldn't be so calm. She's a good weather vane where Marian is concerned."

Hattie had opened the drapes at the French windows, but there was little to see outside through the rain. Water pattered onto Marian's newly painted chairs and tabletops, and formed pools in low spots on the patio. Glistening droplets clung to the undersides of chairs. Through the rain I could make out the big white X Marian had painted below her window.

After lunch I finished the accounts and turned off the computer.

"All done?" Jason asked, looking up from one of his farming bulletins. "Write yourself a check. We haven't paid you in over a month."

"I don't really need money while I'm here."

"True, but it's money owed you. Let's keep the record straight." He signed a blank check and passed the checkbook to me. "What are you planning to do afterward, Kate?

"Pay off my debts. If there's anything left, I'd like to travel, in a low-key budget way."

"I've traveled," he said, putting it in the past. "It wasn't the way I had dreamed, though. When I was younger and free, I was poor. When I acquired money, encumbrances came with it. Someday I'll be free again and have the money I need, but by then I won't be young and active." He gave a quick laugh at the irony of it. "It's rather like *Alice in Wonderland*. Nothing seems to work out just right and it's always been that way, even when I was a child."

I said nothing, hoping he would continue so I could get some insight into the other half of this marriage.

"My father was a drunk," he sighed. "The official term is alcoholic, but to me he was a drunk, a miserable failure of a man. My mother never let him forget it either. She didn't scream or accuse him, but her martyred silence made a worse accusation. It said so clearly that while he had failed, she was still standing by him, holding his head when he was sick, making do with almost nothing, a fine woman who deserved better."

"I mean, what can you do with martyrdom?" he implored. "It's the most corrosive of all qualities to live with, because if you push back, the martyr just stands there stoically, and you're left being the bad guy. I saw it eat into my father's soul. She'd hold his hand and look at him with mournful, understanding eyes and murmur, 'Poor Edward. Don't worry, darling. Tomorrow things will be better.' Only tomorrow they were always worse.

"My mother taught piano lessons and took in sewing and alterations to pay for things, and was always thin and overworked, with red strained eyes. She had a cough that always sounded like an accusation of my father. Sometimes in the night I'd hear her cough until I was willing to do anything to make her stop. I wondered why my father didn't do something, but he was a coward. Finally he died and escaped her and everything else, and I was glad for him."

He looked at me as if he'd just realized I was there, listening to his tirade. He seemed to be looking right through me, back to another time, other women.

"Then she turned on me. My father had failed her, but I was not going to, no matter what she had to do. I was her hope of achieving the status and wealth she thought she—and I—deserved. I was in high school then, in a big school where I could hide out in a crowd. I was a square on a seating chart, a name in grade books, member of no clubs. I was average and I accepted it, but my mother talked incessantly about how brilliant I was and what a splendid career I had ahead of me. She never narrowed it to a specific field, but whatever I chose, it was going to be glorious."

He paused to tamp down the tobacco in his pipe and relight it. As he talked it had gone out. He went on, recalling, his eyes distant. "Of course I couldn't be expected to reach my full potential or meet the right people in a public school, so she enrolled me in a prestigious private school—at great sacrifice to herself, which she never let me forget. To her dying day she reminded me of how much I had to be grateful for, and forced gratitude can be very debilitating. It's a chain that grows shorter and shorter until finally it chokes out love." His voice was brittle with bitterness.

As he talked he'd been pacing before the fireplace, pausing to poke at the dying embers. We didn't need a fire on a spring afternoon, but it was inviting. He turned suddenly to me and said, "I don't know why I'm burdening you with all this. Except it's been bottled up and fermenting, and you've touched the right switch to release it all."

"It's no burden," I said. "I'm willing to listen to both you and Marian. It sounds like you had similar childhoods, with high expectations from your parents that you didn't feel you could meet."

"I suppose you're right," he said, as if the similarity had never occurred to him. He smiled slightly, then continued. "When my mother died—just before I graduated from college—I was left with cultured tastes but no money to satisfy them. I enjoyed the right food and wine, I appreciated the right music and art, I dressed well and I could carry on a high-level conversation. Those talents would have qualified me as a paid escort on a ship and not much more, so that's what I became for a time. I deliberately set out to marry for money, and a top-of-the-line cruise ship was a place to meet wealthy single women. It wasn't exactly the glorious career my mother had envisioned for me, but it was something I knew I could accomplish.

"I'd studied women, beginning with my mother, and I realized that most women want drama in a relationship, not calm companionship. They are attracted to the bad boys, not the nice ones. They enjoy being subdued and even mistreated. But they think they can reform the bad boy. Many of the world's famous 'great lovers' were cads but they were handsome charmers who managed to make the right woman aware of them at the right time. Some of those great lovers were actually vicious, but they had an air of unattainability so that women were challenged. Each one thought that she alone could understand and satisfy this man, so he'd finally be happy, but then, if he were happy, she'd never have wanted him. It's like women aren't satisfied until they have obliterated whatever it was that attracted them in the first place." His voice was like a dull knife scraping on metal.

"Whoa, that's not true!" I burst out. "It's usually the other way around." I thought of Harold, who had almost destroyed me, taking away my self-confidence, my joyful spirit and eventually my self-respect before he grew bored with me and left.

Jason came out of his reverie and stared at me, almost as if I were a stranger who had come upon him naked. I think he already regretted telling me too much. "Perhaps not you personally, Kate. I was just saying 'most women,' and it's certainly true of Marian."

"But she loves you," I protested.

He laughed harshly. "She fell in love with an imaginary hero, not with me. She couldn't see me for the huge halo she placed on my head. Unfortunately, everyday living dulls the shine. I'm not perfect, and when she began to realize I lacked the qualities she'd endowed me with, she began to chip away at what there was of the real me."

"Like what?"

"I never told her I could jump fences on horseback, yet she feels cheated that I can't. She'd like a dashing, romantic man who also has the business savvy to manage Marbury Hill profitably. I'm trying, but the place barely makes ends meet when it should be showing a good return. She hates me, but I've done nothing but try my best, just like I did for Joanna." He added the last part softly, and I wasn't sure he was aware he had said it out loud.

I hadn't asked to hear all this, and yet I couldn't stop listening and walk away. I got up and poured coffee from the silver pot Hattie had left, though I knew the coffee would be cold. It was something to do. My hands shook so that I slopped coffee over the side of Jason's cup, right onto his hands.

Still engrossed with his story, he didn't seem to notice the spill. "I suppose it would have been better for Marian in the long run if I'd just been the paid escort. Then we'd both have been free to leave the relationship whenever it stopped satisfying us. But for a woman in her position, never married, with a family like hers, it was unthinkable. And I didn't really want to just be paid for my services. One thing my mother instilled in me that I appreciate is propriety. I knew that Marian had a bit of money, but she wasn't and isn't wealthy enough to keep us cruising on the six-star ships in the top deck suite, or owning half a dozen homes or being chauffeured about in a Rolls. So whatever you and anyone else might think, I didn't marry Marian for her money. If I had, it would have been a very low bid on my part. I had other reasons."

"So you must have loved her." Only after I'd said it did I realize I'd spoken in the past tense: 'must have loved her', not 'must love her.'

"I must have," he said, shaking his head. "But it feels like that love has faded away and left nothing, not trust or companionship. I suppose at first my air of sophistication impressed her. I'd been around more than she had, but that wasn't saying much. I was used to saying the right things, and it worked. I was her first love—except for that damn cousin of hers—and she still thinks of me that way, like a teenager would, including all the dramatic stunts."

He paused, drained his coffee cup, then continued. "There's something immensely appealing about the purity of a child's innocent adoration. When she thought of me as a hero, I wanted to be one. I wanted to protect her illusions, protect her from the harsh realities of the world, protect her even from her despair and suicidal thoughts. You probably feel the same way about her, don't you? Otherwise you wouldn't have stayed after the snow melted."

I nodded, though he was only partially right. I'd stayed for Marian, and because I liked the ease and luxury of life at Marbury Hill, but there was also a reason or two that I didn't want to admit.

He sighed, looked at his empty coffee cup and set it down. "Let's have some music," he said, going to the TV and pressing a few buttons. "This sound system is one of the few extravagances I've permitted myself with her money. What would you like to hear?"

"I don't care. Something suitable for a rainy day." I went to the French window and stared out into the rain. The rain had declined to a mist, and the white walls of Marbury Hill looked wavering and mysterious.

"Perhaps 'Water Music' or the bit from the Sorcerer's Apprentice where everything gets flooded." We both chuckled slightly.

A moment later vibrant, stirring chords filled the room. "Ah, Beethoven," I said.

"Which?" Jason asked, close beside me.

"Fifth. Next question?"

"How do you feel about me?"

"I … can't answer that."

"Can't? Or won't?"

"There's a different answer every day, and I don't know which is correct." I glanced upward toward Marian's window and saw a moving curtain and a blur of gold. Marian was watching the library window, watching us. I stepped away from Jason, evading his arms and his nearness. "What other music do you have?" I asked, though at that moment music was totally unimportant.

"I have a lot of piano music. I used to play." He flexed his fingers.

"Will you play for me? Is there a piano here? I haven't seen one."

"In the music room."

"I haven't been in there. Marian stopped me."

"She won't like hearing me play. That's one reason I haven't played since you've been here."

"Why doesn't she like it? You can't be that bad." I tried to turn it into a joke, to relieve the tension between us.

"Marian never learned to play, despite lessons and forced practice, but her mother was an excellent pianist, according to Marian. Let's be brave and open the music room."

I followed him and took a seat in a small upholstered chair where I could watch his hands as he played.

He touched the keys tentatively, as if feeling for a melody lurking there, ran a few experimental scales. "It's out of tune," he announced, as he began Grieg's Piano Concerto.

I heard footsteps as Marian ran into the room. She slammed down the piano lid, almost crushing Jason's hands. "How dare you?!" she screamed. Then, without even glancing at me, she fled back upstairs.

Wordlessly, Jason stalked back to the library. He flipped the CD player back on, turned up the volume as loud as it would go and threw open the library door. The music crashed against the walls and shrieked up the stairway, pounding at the ancient walls. Jason leaned against the window frame and laughed.

I shut off the music and ran to my room, but I could still hear his laughter, and in my mind, the music as well.

They're mad, I thought. *They're both mad. They have the same twisted kind of past that makes them want to destroy each other, and if I stay here I'll go mad too.*

Chapter 10

I stayed in my room the rest of the afternoon. *Leave Marbury Hill,* the rational part of my brain insisted. *Run, now, today, while you still can.* I dragged my suitcase out of the closet, flung it onto the bed and began taking clothing off hangers to pack. But my hands slowed. I knew it was already too late for me to escape. Where would I go? And what would I do once I got there? My bank account was almost empty, and Jason would almost certainly stop payment on my check as soon as I left.

No, I was caught by Jason and Marian, caught like a child staring at fire, fascinated by the light and flickering, changing flame, but knowing that fire can burn and destroy. I would stay to see things to the end, even if I got burned. I hung the clothing back in the closet and stowed the suitcase away once more. But for the first time, I asked Hattie to send Nate up with my supper on a tray. I didn't want to see either of the Ashbys. If I got fired for dereliction of duty, so be it. That would force my decision.

Sunlight streaming through my window awoke me the next morning. We'd all be better off out in the sunshine than cooped up inside agitating each other.

As I came downstairs, I saw that the parlor door was tightly closed, and I knew that the door to the music room was too, and probably locked. There would be no more piano playing.

Both Ashbys were already at breakfast, Jason silent and withdrawn, Marian sullen and making a great show of clinking silverware and clicking her cup as she set it into the saucer, things she knew annoyed Jason. They both wore outdoor clothes. It was unusual for the two of them to be up ahead of me, and to be dining together.

I took the last of the scrambled eggs and the remaining two hot rolls, poured myself coffee and sat down. Hattie hadn't brought breakfast trays. How had she known not to?

No one mentioned the previous day's events. That seemed to be a pattern and I should have been used to it by then. Each day was to be endured separately, with little relation to the past or the future. Whatever happened simply happened, and I could only brace myself for what might happen next.

"I'd like to go into town," I said, breaking the silence. "Would you like to go along, Marian?"

"No. People stare at me. Besides, we need to finish getting the flowerbeds ready. You can buy some plants in town," she suggested with excitement.

"I can go and pick up whatever you need," Jason said.

"No, I want to do some shopping. For feminine things." I was almost certain that would put him off, and I was right.

"Very well," he conceded. He pushed his plate back. "Shall we get those flowerbeds in order first?"

I was astonished that he'd even consider outdoor work, and apparently so was Marian. She gave him a puzzled, suspicious look, but then smiled and stood, ready to go out. "I have a few things to do in the office first," he said. "I'll join you in a bit."

"I knew he wouldn't really do any work," Marian said as we walked to the summer house. The farmhands had cleaned out the stable and left a wheelbarrow and two bagfuls of manure in the summer house to be used in the flowerbeds. I trundled a load down to the sunken garden with Marian strolling beside me, not offering to help. I dumped it and headed back to the summer house, leaving Marian out in the sunshine.

Jason appeared at my side. "Where's Marian?" he demanded.

"She was right outside." Only she wasn't any more.

"Why did you let her out of your sight?"

"There she is." I pointed to where Marian was running toward the stable. "Wait, Marian!" I called.

"Hang on! We can all go riding!" Jason added.

"I don't believe you," Marian spat at him. She paused, out of breath, beside a pile of rocks the workers had picked up and left for us to use in edging the flowerbeds.

When Jason got close to her, Marian grabbed up a handful of rocks and turned to face us. "Don't come near me, Jason."

As he edged forward, she hurled a rock, hitting him on the chest. She threw another and another, amazingly accurate. I watched, horrified, as one after the other hit and brought blood. Jason kept walking toward her, blood streaming down his shirt front. Marian suddenly dropped the rest of the rocks and ran for the stable, slamming the door behind her.

I caught up with Jason and reached to touch his wounds.

He jerked away. "No, I'm fine. Help me get the door open."

We threw our weight against the door. I felt it give and heard Marian hit the floor with a thud. As we went in, she grabbed a pitchfork and backed against Jeff's stall. "Don't touch me, Jason, or I'll stick this right through you," she threatened. "I know you want to kill me."

"Marian, Jason cares about you," I said. "I care about you. Please put that down."

In the instant she turned toward me, Jason wrenched the pitchfork from her and flung it aside, then tried to control her flailing arms. He struck Marian across the face and she slumped sobbing into his arms.

Jason and I each took an arm and half-led, half-carried her up to the house. By the time we got her to her room she'd calmed and was quiet.

"I'm going to give you a sedative, Marian," Jason said. "And I think I'd better lock you in so you won't try anything else stupid."

"I won't run away, Jason. Don't lock me in. I can't stand it!"

Her words wrung pity from me, until I saw her eyes. They were watching Jason, sizing him up, crafty eyes that glittered with hatred. After all, if he had the key on the outside, he was in control.

"Stay with her while I go for the sedative," Jason commanded me.

When he'd gone she said in a wounded voice, "You're not nice. I'm sorry I told Adam you were."

Jason returned with two of the small yellow pills and a glass of water, and watched while Marian swallowed them. She flung an angry look at me as I tucked her into bed, but she said nothing more to me.

After Jason locked the door and we started downstairs, I said, "I feel kind of responsible for—"

"Forget it." He cut me off. "We've both got to be more careful. She's been in so much better spirits since you came that I'd gotten complacent. I should have known it couldn't last."

"We've got to tend your wounds. You could have an infection from those dirty rocks. Where do you keep the first aid kit?"

"In my bathroom, locked away from Marian. I'll get it."

"I can come along. It would save time."

"No. I'll get it."

While waiting for him to bring the kit into the library, I wondered if he was being overly secretive about his room and if there was something in there he didn't want me to see. *You're starting to sound like Marian*, I thought.

He sat in the big chair by the window and leaned back, flinching as I dabbed at his cuts with rubbing alcohol.

As I finished dressing his wounds, he reached up and pulled my face down close to his. I turned to one side and whispered, "No, Jason."

Abruptly he let me go and as I straightened, I looked out to the patio. Marian's slashing white cross was still there, marking the spot. I looked up to her window and saw her standing there watching us, not in bed as we'd left her. I whirled to tell Jason, but he'd already guessed. "She was bound to find out how I felt about you some time, Kate. It's hard to hide … love." He gave the last word a soft inflection and widened his eyes as he said it.

"But this isn't love," I stammered. "I don't even know what this is." Before he could say anything more, I fled for the kitchen. Hattie wasn't there, but I found the ice cubes I sought, wrapped them in a dish towel and went back to the library. I handed the icy bundle to Jason, not willing to touch him.

"I still want to go into town," I said.

"I can take you. Marian is safely locked in, and Hattie will check on her."

"I could really use some alone time," I said firmly, wondering why he didn't trust me to go into town. "Is there a car I can drive, or should I call a taxi?"

"We have two cars. As soon as you get changed, come down and I'll take you to the garage. I keep it locked too."

"I'll ask Marian if she needs anything. May I have the key to her room?"

When I went in she was standing by the window, looking down at the patio, at her white cross. I went to stand beside her and I could see down into the library. I imagined what she'd seen when Jason tried to kiss me. "Have you come to gloat?" she asked.

"Why would I gloat? I'm sorry you're locked up. It's my fault. I should have been watching you."

"I've been watching you too, you and Jason."

I ignored her remark, for I had no defense. "I'm going into town. What flowers should I buy for the beds?"

"Get whatever you want."

"But it's your house and your garden."

"Is it? Is anything mine outside of this room?"

I was feeling the familiar irritated impatience Marian could bring out, but I reminded myself that I'd been hired to look after her, and on this day I'd failed. "I think I'll get impatiens for the shady spots and several shades of petunias," I suggested. "They'll bloom all summer, after I'm gone."

"Kate, you can't go! What will I do without you? We can have fun, especially when Adam comes back. We can go riding and swimming and play tennis. And it's beautiful here in the fall. We can go looking for walnuts and gather up colored leaves and dried pods to make decorations. Wouldn't you like that?"

It was another of Marian's 180-degree mood changes. "That does sound like fun," I said, promising nothing. I couldn't make any far-reaching plans, but I was relieved that she was taking an interest in getting outside again, so I used it to my advantage. "We can have a vegetable garden too. I'll pick up some seeds." I named vegetables, trying to remember what had been in my grandfather's garden: corn, beans, lettuce, radishes.

"Radishes are for children."

"Then we won't have radishes. We can have whatever you want."

"Stop patronizing me."

"All right," I sighed. "If you want something, say so. If not, I've got to be on my way."

"Paperback books, chocolates, nail polish and lots of makeup. I want to look pretty before I die."

"Will you please stop talking about dying! I'm tired of hearing it." Then I said something I'd come to regret: "If you're so intent on dying, go on and get it over with."

When I saw the shocked look on her face, I tried to mollify my remark. "Okay, then I assume that you're going to live and that you'll want to go outside. So, would you like to have jeans or shorts, or maybe a wraparound skirt?"

"Yes, all of it."

She could easily afford several wardrobes, so I wrote down all three clothing options. As I turned to leave, she said, "Kate, get me a surprise."

"What kind of surprise?"

"If I choose, it won't be a surprise. Choose whatever you think I'd like. And when you get back, I may have a surprise for you."

"Is it Adam? Is he back?" My heart leaped at the thought of seeing him again.

"I don't think so. I'll call him if Jason lets me have my phone." I turned away to hide my disappointment and the realization that even if he were home, he hadn't called me.

Chapter 11

When Jason unlocked the garage and keyed in a code to open the door, I could see inside the shapes of two cars, both covered with tarps. He flung the cover off the one nearest the door, a sporty black two-seater BMW.

"Marian bought this as a wedding gift, and we drove it across the country. It needs to be taken out for a run from time to time, but we haven't gone driving in a good while." He ran his hand appreciatively over the gleaming hood.

"I wouldn't feel right driving that, Jason."

"Oh, don't worry, you're not going to. It takes some getting used to, and after all the rain we've had you might run into a muddy spot." He flung the tarp off the other car, a midsize sedan, several years old, gray and anything but sporty. "This one hasn't been taken out lately either." He handed me a credit card. "There's enough gasoline in it to get you into town, but not much more. Go by the Exxon station just as you get into town and fill up, and have somebody check the tire pressure. They're probably all low."

He opened the car door and got in. "I'll back it out for you. Take it easy until you get used to the car and our roads, especially crossing the bridge over the creek."

"I remember it. I'll be careful."

He got out, leaving the car in Park with the motor running. I got in and backed slowly out to turn around, conscious that he was watching me.

As soon as I pulled the chain and drove out through the gate, I felt as if a weight had been lifted from me. Despite its age and stodgy appearance, the car ran smoothly. I found the steering a little stiff, but I got accustomed to it. I glanced at Adam's mailbox, but it was closed with the flag down, so of course I couldn't determine whether he was home or not. I put the windows down, turned on the radio and enjoyed being free and away from all the tension and stress of Marbury Hill. It was my first time away, and it was to be the last happy day I had for a long time.

As I headed down the curving hilly road toward the bridge, I pumped the brakes and felt my foot go too close to the floor. I managed to get the car into second gear, which slowed it down enough for me to maneuver across the bridge, but just barely. I stopped just beyond the other end and went back to look down the sheer rock face from the roadway to the stream. The water rippled and shimmered in the sunlight, tumbling over rocks and forming a whirlpool downstream. The bridge smelled of tar and wet sand, and felt rough where I leaned my arms on the gritty rail. I fished a penny out of my purse and tossed it backward over my shoulder into the stream, whispering a fervent prayer, *Let all this trouble be over soon.*

I longed to stay where I was, alone and peaceful, but I made myself drive on into town.

Following Jason's directions, I pulled into the Exxon station, and was pumping gas into the tank when I heard a familiar voice. "Well, Kate Flynn, I see you've stuck it out longer than I expected. Or are you running away even as we speak?"

"As you speak," I said, "I'm not running away, just running errands."

He came over and took the handle from me. "Let me do that. So, there's not been any big trouble?"

"No more than usual." I could hardly accept how glad I was to see him, and I didn't want to waste any more time talking about the Ashbys. I wanted to hear what he was doing, and where he'd been.

"That can mean anything," he said with a grin. The pump shut off, he replaced it and handed me the receipt.

"Can you do me a favor, Adam? I need to have the tire pressure checked."

"Glad to." He pulled the car over to the air hose, and I could tell by the dings that he was putting in a lot of air. He backed, turned and brought the car to a stop beside me. "Did you see the Beamer?"

I nodded. "But I wasn't allowed to drive it."

"I'm glad."

"Is there something wrong with it?"

"No, but he might think that letting you drive it would mean you owed him."

"Then I'm glad too."

"Tell you what: I have errands of my own to run. I'll meet you in the parking lot of the old courthouse and take you to lunch." He pointed to where I saw a golden dome gleaming in the sunlight.

"What time?"

"Whoever finishes first waits for the other."

When I presented the check Jason had given me to the bank teller, she studied it a moment, went for her supervisor and came back to say I'd have to open an account. I did, keeping out $100 in cash.

I hadn't realized until I went into a busy department store just how much I'd missed seeing ordinary people and things, not the faded antiquity of Marbury Hill. I wandered along counters looking at shiny new items until the cashier must have thought I was shoplifting, or casing the place for a robbery. I got a cart and began to fill it with Marian's requests: sneakers, socks, jeans, shorts, a denim dress with a sailor collar. Marian would like that, I decided. She was always talking about ships.

I still needed a gift for her, but I didn't know what. She already had everything a woman could want—and yet nothing of real value. In the fabric department I saw a bolt of lavender linen and bought three yards, a simple pattern, a zipper and thread. Together we could make Marian an attractive new dress. Lavender would look good on her. As I passed the perfume counter I added a bottle of lilac fragrance cologne. I remembered that fragrance from Marian's mother's room. I put all the purchases on Jason's credit card.

At the hardware store I bought two flats of plants, a handful of packets of seeds and a small container of general purpose fertilizer. "Ten-ten-ten is what you want," the clerk said. He rang up my purchases and stowed them in the trunk of the car.

The pharmacy was the last stop. I chose five paperback romances after only a cursory glance at the titles. I didn't remember reading any of them, though I could have. I doubted if Marian would remember either. I chose eye shadow, eyebrow pencil, foundation, and several shades of lipstick and nail polish. When I took my purchases to checkout, I reached again for the credit card and my finger touched the pill I'd found under Marian's pillow. I laid it on the counter and asked the pharmacist if he knew what it was.

He turned it over carefully. "Nothing I recognize. We don't stock it here. Could you have ordered it from Canada or some other online company?"

"I didn't buy it, but I'd like to know what's in it. It made someone sick. I'll pay you for your analysis."

"No charge. I'm intrigued. I can't give you an answer today, though. We're backed up on prescriptions, and I'd have to look it up in the PDR."

"PDR?"

"Physicians Desk Reference. Lists all kinds of drugs by color, ingredients, uses and names. Tells side effects too. Can you check back in about a week?"

I said I could.

When I came in sight of the courthouse I saw Adam leaning against his pickup, his long legs crossed. He waved when he saw me and started walking toward the car. "Lock all your purchases in the trunk of the car and come ride with me. I don't want to ride in anything that Jason Ashby's occupied."

I followed him to the pickup. "Any particular reason?"

"Because seeing you in that car reminds me that you're there at Marbury Hill with him and not with me."

"You could have called me."

"I tried twice, but each time Jason answered and said you weren't available and neither was Marian. I started to drive over and see for myself, but I thought that might just cause trouble. You never walked down by the river again either."

"You could have called my cell."

"You never gave me your number. You had mine. Why didn't you call me?"

I turned to him in surprise. "I thought you knew my number."

"How would I know? I'm not the NSA."

I laughed. "That's fair. Still, you left so quickly after dinner that night that I thought something was wrong. And you didn't say why you were going away or for how long."

"I have a broker's office in Richmond. I do a lot of work by computer, but every so often I need to show up in person to remind everyone that I'm still alive. Things come up that sometimes keep me longer than I expect. Plus I flew down to Florida to a timeshare I have there, trying to get you out of my mind."

"But why?" I was so glad to see him that I wanted to throw my arms around him and breathe in the smell of him, and he hadn't even said he'd missed me.

"I want you when you're free and clear of everything that's going on in that house," he said, looking at me sadly, "and I don't think you will be for a while." I felt a slight chill and wondered if he somehow knew about the tug-of-war I'd had with myself over whether or not to leave. He offered me his arm, and we walked into the inn.

It had been a grist mill years earlier, and the huge water wheel still turned slowly in a stream at the side of the building, while ducks bobbed in the pond that fed the millrace. Inside was dark and cool, with rough-hewn trestle tables and broad board flooring. A potted red geranium stood on each gingham-covered tabletop.

"I like this," I said.

"I thought you would." His voice was warm, and so was his hand at the small of my back as he guided me to a table.

"I hope the food is as good as the décor."

"If you're dissatisfied, or still hungry afterward, we'll go to my cabin and heat up some of last night's leftovers."

We ordered Italian. It wasn't as good as Hattie's food, but I didn't care. Adam sat across the rustic table from me, smiled and talked about ordinary things. "Do you want to talk about what's been going on at Marbury Hill?" he asked.

"I'll tell you a little, and then hopefully we can put it behind us." I told him about Marian's outburst and the pitchfork incident.

"She's all over the map lately," Adam mused. "Do you think she might be on some kind of drugs?"

"I hadn't thought about that. But where would she get them?"

He didn't answer that. "Why don't I drop by the house when she's not expecting me and see how she acts? I'll take that box she told you about, too. That seems to prey on her mind."

"Thanks."

"Sometimes I think that marriage is only going to end with one of them dead," he said sadly. "But I'm not sure what either of us can do about it, so we shouldn't dwell on it. I just want to enjoy dining with an attractive woman, no angst, no drama, no pitchforks." He winked at me and I smiled at him.

He talked about his business, his farm, his dog Shep, and asked me about books I'd read, where I liked to travel, if I might like to spend time in Florida. It was wonderful, and time passed far too quickly. His eyes no longer seemed mocking or threatening, but soothing, like gray velvet, or fur. I noticed how strong and tanned his hands were and how comforting I felt in his presence.

"Dessert at my place?" he asked.

"I'm not at all hungry, but I'd love to go to your place." I tried to make this sound flirty rather than sleazy; I think I pulled it off.

"That's my kind of woman. I doubt if I could scratch up any dessert anyway." When he opened the car door for me, he said, "Be careful of that bridge."

"I remembered it from the day I arrived, so I put the car in a lower gear coming down the hill. The brakes seemed soft."

"People have gone off the end into the creek," he said. "Including Marian's mother, Aunt Olivia."

I had the key in the ignition, but I turned it off to look at him. "Is that how she died? Marian never said."

He nodded. "Nobody in the family talked about it, not after the first shock. She was going to meet another man, leaving Uncle Angus and Marian. He went on a weeklong bender, and you know what happened to Marian." He closed the car door, leaned in through the window to lightly kiss my cheek and said, "Follow me."

He pulled off and I followed. He slowed for the bridge and we both navigated it safely. We'd almost reached the drive to his house when an ambulance went screaming past. We both pulled to the side, and at that moment my cell phone rang. It was Jason. "Kate, come home immediately. There's been an accident."

Chapter 12

I signaled Adam and pulled out, following the ambulance to Marbury Hill. I knew something had happened to Marian. It never occurred to me that it might have been someone else—not Hattie or Nate, or Jason himself.

I left the car in front of the garage and ran for the front door, where Hattie was getting into the ambulance. I heard her say, "It's down beyond the stable," as the door slid closed and the ambulance pulled off, spraying gravel. Adam parked behind me and we ran together down the lane.

By the time we reached the accident site, a paramedic was squatting beside Marian, checking her vital signs and calling out numbers to his partner, who relayed them to the hospital.

Marian lay sprawled just behind the shattered gate that led to the bridle path. Her face was as pale as plaster against a hideous flowing robe. What was she doing down in the woods in her robe? And without shoes? One arm was twisted under her, and her hair was spread out like hemp drying in the sunlight. Marian's chest moved slightly with each breath, making the orange chiffon flutter. She resembled a great orange bird that had plunged to the forest floor and landed on a bed of pine needles. A cluster of tiny yellow butterflies fluttered about the gate, and flies buzzed, drawn by blood. I heard a crow caw off in the distance, and Jeff nicker in the stable.

Jason sat on the ground opposite the paramedic, holding her hand, his face drawn with anguish. "I haven't moved her," he said.

"Good. We're equipped for it. You're not."

"Where are you taking her?" Jason asked.

"The hospital, of course."

"Can't you treat her here?"

The paramedic stared at Jason in astonishment. "Good God, man, no. I'm not a doctor, and she may have serious internal injuries. We won't know until we see the scans, but that arm is definitely broken."

Jason stood. "Of course. I wasn't thinking."

The paramedics lifted Marian onto a stretcher, tucked a blanket about her and lifted her into the ambulance. "May I ride with you?" Jason asked.

"We're expecting you to. You're the nearest of kin, aren't you? You'll be needed to supply a lot of information."

They had already started the engine as Jason clambered in and turned to say, "Kate, pack an overnight bag for Marian and bring it when you come to pick me up." Only then did he notice Adam beside me, and a look of distaste passed across his face. Then the ambulance door slammed shut and the vehicle moved off up the lane.

Hattie muttered, "I should have gone along in the ambulance with her, not him."

"He's nearest of kin," Adam reminded her.

"You are, not him. He's been nothing but trouble ever since Miss Marian laid eyes on him and brought him here. And it won't let up until he's got Miss Marian resting in her grave. That poor child…"

"What happened, Hattie?" I asked.

"I'm not really sure. First thing I know, Mr. Ashby come running into the kitchen, screaming at me, 'Where is Miss Marian?' She done got out, and we got to find her. He say I left the door unlocked when I took her some lemonade and cookies and I told him I didn't, but there ain't no call to keep her locked up in her own home nohow. He said 'No time for jabber. We got to find her.'"

She sighed and went on, "I knew well enough where she'd be. Ever since she was a little girl she's gone riding when she was upset. Mr. Ashby knew it too. He headed straight for the stable. When we got halfway there we saw Miss Marian lead Jeff out of the stable, jump on and go tearing away. Jeff was rearing and carrying on like he was possessed, and I was prepared for the worst. In a minute we heard a crash and a scream. When we got here she was laying just like you saw her. Mr. Ashby sent me to the house to call the Rescue Squad and bring his phone while he stayed with her, but it ought to have been the other way around. Miss Marian always felt easy around me."

Hattie had never been so talkative around me before. I realized it was Adam's presence. She was angry at being accused of neglecting Marian, and hurt at being excluded when Marian needed her.

"Marian's going to be all right," Adam said with far more assurance than I felt.

Hattie shook her head. "No, she ain't. She going to die. I've had the signs."

"What signs?" Adam asked.

Her face closed against us, like dark shutters drawn. She'd said more than she intended. "Nothing white folks care about," she concluded.

"What about Jeff?" I asked, averting my eyes from the smashed gate and the pool of blood drying on the ground in front of it."

"Nate's working on him," she said. "He's always loved that horse, almost as much as Miss Marian did, ever since he was tiny."

We started walking up the lane toward the stable. Where the lane divided, Hattie went toward the house, but I felt drawn to the stable. Adam touched my arm, warning me away. "He may have some ugly wounds."

I felt compelled to see the horse, despite his wounds. If I saw Marian's horse, I might somehow understand why she felt compelled to ride him.

Nate was stroking Jeff's face, trying to calm the frantic horse. He'd tied Jeff to the stall door and Lucas leaned against Jeff's rump, keeping him stable. The horse shifted nervously and neighed with shrill fear every time Nate touched his wounds with wet compresses. Jeff's coat was sticky with blood, and two sharp points of wood protruded from his chest, like banderillos in a bull. As I looked, Nate pulled out one of the wood splinters, bringing a clot and a gush of fresh blood. Jeff kicked furiously, knocking Lucas to the floor.

"Did you call a vet?" Adam asked.

"We didn't have no time yet. Miss Marian had to come first," Nate said. "Easy, Jeff. Nice Jeff," he soothed, his dark hand moving down the horse's neck. "I'm gonna fix you up and take care of you, Jeff."

I started to tell him it was no use. Even if Jeff had no broken bones and got no infections from his wounds, Jason would have him put down. I felt sick with the knowledge. Adam, observant, pulled me against him, shielding me from the sight of the injured horse.

"Something was wrong with Jeff today," Nate said. "Before this, I mean. Jeff was acting wild, not like himself. I tried to tell Miss Marian."

"Marian should have known better than to ride Jeff if something was wrong with him," I said, puzzled.

"Who knows why Marian does anything?" Adam said ruefully. "Come away, Kate. You can't help here, and you've got to pack that bag."

As we walked toward the house, Jeff's agonized cries followed me. I made myself think of Marian, imagining her astride Jeff, her orange robe bright against his dark glossy coat as they tore joyfully down the lane toward the gate, I envisioned Marian crying out, "Go, Jeff! Jump!" and anticipating the momentary thrill at soaring over the gate and landing like a dancer on the other side. Then Jeff, exerting himself far beyond what a horse his age should do, trying desperately to please his beloved mistress and clear that gate. Stumbling, perhaps. Or leaping as he knew how to do, but without the spring of youth, crashing into the gate, bringing it down with him, Marian tossed over his head. Or had he been drugged or sick, as Nate suggested?

"What can I do to help?" Adam asked, breaking into my reverie.

"Go with me to the hospital. I don't want to be alone with Jason."

"Neither would I," he muttered.

"It will take me only a few minutes to pack a bag for Marian. Can you unload the car? Set the plants out there anywhere, and the fertilizer, and bring the rest of the things inside."

The door to Marian's room was ajar, and her belongings were scattered in their usual disarray so that I half expected her to call my name. Her bed was rumpled, her hairbrush lay full of hair on the dresser and a paperback was opened face down on the bedside table. Why had she gone out so abruptly? Had she heard Jeff's irresistible nicker through the open window? And Jason had given her two of the sedatives. Why hadn't they worked? Or were they something else entirely? I couldn't answer any of those questions.

As I finished packing night clothes, slippers and her toiletries, Adam came upstairs laden with my purchases, the purple-wrapped cologne atop the heap of packages like some garish ornament. "Where do all these go?"

"In here. They're all for Marian."

"You didn't buy anything for yourself?"

"No. The wrapped gift goes in my room. Marian asked me to bring her a surprise, and that's it. She said she'd have one for me in return."

"Well, I guess you could say she did, but it wasn't a good one." He piled the packages onto Marian's chair and turned to me. "You should leave this place. Now."

"And leave Marian?"

"Yes. And Jason."

"And you?"

"Who said anything about that?" he responded, gathering me into a hug that I hadn't realized I needed.

We closed the window and left, closing the door behind us.

"You don't want to take the gift to the hospital for her?" he asked when I set it in my room.

"No, they'll probably send her home tomorrow."

"Since you didn't buy yourself anything, I should have gotten you a gift."

"Why? You took me to lunch and that was gift enough. You don't owe me anything."

We were silent on the drive into town, in contrast to our easy conversation over lunch. How long had it been since our meeting by the river? It seemed half a lifetime.

We spent an hour in the visitors' lounge at the hospital, leafing through old magazines, glancing occasionally at the TV and at our watches, before Jason came in.

"There's no need for you to wait, Kate," he said, his glance dismissing Adam altogether, as if Adam didn't count and could do whatever he wanted. "There doesn't seem to be any internal injuries, but she'll be kept overnight for observation. Her right wrist is shattered. It will be weeks before she'll have much use of it. When she comes home you'll need to be her nursemaid, as well as doing for her what she normally does with her right hand."

I nodded, accepting the enormity of my new tasks. It meant helping her with almost everything she did: eating, dressing, bathing, brushing her hair, even unwrapping the gift I'd bought her. I couldn't leave now, and that realization brought home to me just how trapped I felt.

He went on and I realized I was only half listening. "Marian's heavily sedated, and there's no telling what she might say or do when she comes out of it. I'm going to stay overnight here. Can you come for us in the morning? I'll call you when they release her."

"Of course." I felt a great wave of sympathy for Jason. His face was pinched and gray, his shoulders slumped with fatigue. He still wore the old work clothes he wore around the farm, and he smelled faintly of the stable. "I'm so sorry. If only I hadn't gone into town."

"Don't blame yourself. I told you to go. You deserved a break from us, God knows. Did you bring Marian's bag?"

"Yes." It was beside my chair and I handed it to him. "Would you like us to go get some overnight things for you?"

"No. It doesn't matter how I look. Marian's health and safety are what's important." He took my hand, held it for what seemed a long time, and said, "Thank you for being here."

Adam and I had barely gotten out of the hospital when he exploded, "That sanctimonious bastard! 'Marian's health and safety are all that matters,'" he mimicked. "And what was up with him holding your hand like that?"

"Adam, he's distressed. Don't you think we could cut him a little slack, just this once?"

"He's not distressed; he's afraid of what she might say about him." He jerked open the car door for me then slammed it shut after I'd gotten in.

"What makes you think that?" I asked as he got in and started the car.

"He admitted it, for one thing. Didn't you hear him? 'There's no telling what she'll say or do'?" he quoted with extra emphasis on the word "say."

"That's true," I admitted. "Still, Marian is in one of the safest places she could be right now, surrounded by medical professionals and a security department. And it sounds like her injuries aren't too bad, so how about we give thanks that she's going to be relatively okay and try not to spend the rest of the night being upset?"

He looked at me as if to argue, then broke into a weary smile. "Agreed. Where are we going? Not to you-know-where. Hattie's in no condition to cook tonight, and I'm in no mood to spend the evening there. So that leaves my cabin. Want to pick up a pizza or buy some steaks to grill?"

"Steaks."

"Good choice. Okay, we need steaks, butter, bread, eggs, bacon, and salad greens."

As he spoke, I was keying the items into my phone to make a list. "Don't you keep any food at your place?"

"Nothing perishable. I'm there so seldom it would spoil. Of course, I could make some changes to those habits if it might encourage a certain lady to visit regularly." After a moment he added, "I feel guilty for staying away and not checking on Marian more often. I still think she's unbalanced, but even crazy people can be telling the truth sometimes." He raised his hand. "Sorry. That just slipped out. I swear I won't mention our forbidden topic again."

But we'll both be thinking about it, I thought.

Grass grew uncut around Adam's cabin, and wildflowers bloomed in profusion. As we drove up, rabbits scampered to safety and two squirrels chased each other up an old walnut tree. A rope and board swing hung from one of the gnarled limbs, and I had a sudden wish to swing, free like a child again. Shep ran out to meet us and followed Adam as he unlocked the door and motioned me in.

"Who looks after Shep when you're away?"

"If I'm going to be away overnight, I take him with me. Otherwise, he fends for himself. Don't worry, there's plenty of small game around here; he'd never go hungry." The dog had looked at me when I mentioned his name, then back to Adam, as if he understand he was being discussed. He dropped down by a leather chair, seemingly pleased to be inside.

The cabin had been a tobacco barn, with thick logs running the length of the building. Inside, one end had been partitioned off for a bathroom and a kitchen, with a sleeping loft above. Windows were cut into the logs at intervals, and a huge rock fireplace built along the back wall where the original fireboxes had been. Most of the tier poles that would have held tobacco were still in place, and the main room was a full two stories tall.

"Make yourself at home," Adam called as he stowed the bacon, eggs and milk in the nearly empty fridge and put the other items on the counter beside it. "I told you it was a little austere."

"It's charming," I said, "but doesn't it get awfully cold in the winter?"

"That shows what you know about log barns. I closed the ventilators in the eaves, tacked insulation under the room and put in double windows. Is it cool enough for a fire, you think?"

Without waiting for an answer, he began shredding newspaper and laying sticks and twigs onto the andirons. He lit it and watched as it caught and blazed.

I went toward the fire, needing warmth in the chilly late spring afternoon, but also because I needed to warm my spirits. "Can I help with supper?"

"No thanks. My kitchen's too small for help. I'll make drinks to occupy you until the steaks are done. Are you ravenous?"

"No. Not after our big lunch."

"Good. Then let's walk outside before we eat. It's part of my ritual to check over my property each time I come home. Pride of ownership you might say. I can see changes from week to week."

When we turned toward the door, Shep got up and joined us. We walked along woodland paths and by the edges of meadows lush with silvery green grain. Adam explained how he'd terraced and planted cover crops and pointed out washed out fields where pine seedlings were growing for pulpwood. We came out onto a clearing by the river, and directly across I saw the white bulk of Marbury Hill. Adam said nothing, but turned me back toward his cabin.

"Like swings?" he asked when we were back to the cabin.

I nodded, and sat down on the board, holding the stout ropes. He gave me several hearty pushes, sending me high above the grass and flowers. *This must be how Marian felt when she jumped with Jeff,* I thought, and then resolutely closed off my thoughts of her.

As we went back inside, Adam put his arm companionably about my shoulder, and for a moment I felt secure and normal, like an ordinary woman having dinner with her date instead of someone trying to maintain her sanity in a whirlpool of madness. Then he dropped his arm and headed for the kitchen, returning me to my present condition.

He made whiskey sours and handed me one, nodding toward a kitchen stool near him. "You can sit there and talk to me while I cook. Using the word 'cook' loosely, of course."

Obediently I climbed up and sipped my drink, watching as he washed lettuce and patted it dry with paper towels, arranged steaks on the broiler rack and sprinkled them with garlic salt and pepper, sliced bread and spread butter on it. I liked watching his strong, tanned hands moving over the food, as if he were preparing an offering for me. "Tell me about your job," I said.

"I'm a glorified salesman," he shrugged.

"What do you sell?"

"Stocks and bonds. And I arrange loans for business start-ups."

"Are you a good salesman?"

"One of the best. That's why I'm Vice President of Sales at the firm. In fact, they're sending me to eastern Africa pretty soon. I've been looking forward to it, but I'll miss you." He said it lightly, and I wasn't sure if I should take him seriously.

"Finished your drink?" he asked. "Or do you want to bring it to the table?" He picked up his drink and took a hearty swallow.

"Can I set the table? I've been sitting here doing nothing." I slid down off the stool just as he turned, and our bodies collided. Our eyes met, and for a few seconds, time and motion were suspended. Then he said, "Put the salad on the table," and placed the wooden bowl between us.

I set it on the table and turned back to see him watching me. "Kate," he said softly, and held out his arms to me. I closed the short distance that separated us and lifted my face for the kiss I was expecting and wanting. It was a soft, sweet kiss, and then he held me close and said, "All day I've been wanting to kiss you." Then he stepped back, gave my hand a squeeze and said, "Now let's eat before our steaks are ruined."

They weren't. They were perfect, like everything else about my time at his cabin.

He wouldn't let me help clear away the dishes or wash up. Shep, who'd been waiting patiently throughout the meal, got steak scraps as a reward. I went to the window and looked out toward the woods, where I saw a herd of deer grazing on Adam's lawn. I motioned for him, but by the time he wiped his hands and came to the window, they looked up, saw the motion and fled. Adam got to see only their fleet bodies, white tails in the air, trotting away.

"You missed them," I said.

"I see them nearly every time I'm home. They're my own private herd. No hunting allowed on my property, and they seem to know what those Posted signs mean."

We sat by the fire watching the last embers turn from red to gray. Adam held my hand with one of his, while the other rested on Shep. It was a cozy scene, but it couldn't last.

"I'd better go," I said.

"Stay here."

I glanced around at the big bed, the only one he had.

"We'll make arrangements," he said, interpreting my glance. "I'll be a gentleman."

When I didn't answer, he said, "I don't think you should spend the night all alone over there." He didn't name the place, but of course we knew.

I didn't want to leave, but I was nervous about staying. What would happen? I nodded. "We ought to call Hattie and tell her."

"I'll call. We should have done it sooner. She's probably worried herself into a breakdown." He called and filled Hattie in on what Jason had said, and told her I'd be back in the morning. Then he said, "While I've got the phone on, give me your number. You're not trying to keep it secret, are you?"

"Of course not." I gave him the number. "I keyed yours in that first day. Are you going to call me from Africa?"

"You never know; having each other's numbers may be very important." He said this with more gravity than the rest of our conversation, causing me to wonder what he meant. Then he switched gears. "Hey, I'd better get you to bed. Your eyes are closing. You get first shot at the bathroom."

When I came out of the bathroom, he handed me a nightshirt. "Best I could do on short notice," he said. "It might be a bit big."

I changed while he went to the bathroom, and I wondered if he had condoms stashed somewhere. The nightshirt hung on me like a sack, not at all romantic. I slid into the bed and waited for him.

I wondered what Adam's body would look like. I knew he was fit and muscular from working on his farm, and I'd had his arms around me and his lips on mine. Would he make love to me?

He didn't. He got into the other side of the bed, kissed me lightly, and like the perfect gentleman he'd promised to be, he said goodnight, turned his back on me and fell asleep. I, on the other hand, turned this way and that, unable to give up and sleep. I was torn between relief at not having to deal with the emotions of making love to Adam, and disappointment.

We were having breakfast the next morning when my phone rang. It was Jason. "Marian will be released about eleven-thirty. Can you come for us then?"

"Yes."

Shep whined beside me and Jason heard it. "What was that? I thought I heard a dog. Do you have a dog at Marbury Hill?"

"No. I'm at Adam's."

"Why are you there so early in the morning?"

I started to say it was none of his business, but instead told the truth: "I stayed here last night."

I heard a soft huff and then he said, "We'll talk about this later. Meet us at the front entrance of the hospital. They'll probably bring Marian down the ramp in a wheelchair."

Adam took me to Marbury Hill, much as he'd taken me that first day, driving up to the front porch and dropping me off before he drove away with a wave. I knocked, and when Hattie opened the door she actually allowed me to give her a hug. Then, remembering her job, she closed the door and asked, "Miss Kate, you want some coffee?"

I noted that I had moved up in her approval scale to being called "Miss Kate." Had she finally accepted that I meant no harm to Marian? I was fairly certain that she approved of my spending time with Adam, which had the additional benefit of meaning I wasn't with Jason. I accepted coffee, and then went up to my room to bathe and change clothes before I drove to the hospital. It was a sunny, blissful day, but I couldn't shake off a feeling that something terrible was about to happen—something worse than everything thus far.

Chapter 13

After Jason and I got Marian home and settled in her room, I spent the rest of the afternoon working in the flowerbeds, in sight of her window if she cared to look—and most definitely away from Jason. Despite his somewhat ominous statement that we'd "talk about this," he didn't bring up Adam's name, and neither did I. Each time I checked on Marian, she was asleep. She finally awakened in time for supper, and I helped her downstairs for what turned out to be a silent meal. Marian was still a little groggy, and Jason was pointedly ignoring me.

The next morning I took my gift to Marian, thinking it might cheer her up.

She was awake and lay like a pinioned pink butterfly, her white-wrapped wrist propped helplessly against her chest. Bruises from her fall blotched her face like blue and red crayon marks.

"How do you feel?" I asked gently as I pushed aside the curtains to let in sunlight.

"How do you think I feel? Terrible, that's how! Are you pleased?" she demanded.

"Why should I be pleased? I'm sorry you had a fall and were injured. I'm just glad you weren't hurt more, and that you're back home."

"It was all part of a plan to get rid of me." Her eyes were gray and accusing.

Not again. "Marian, *you* went out and rode Jeff. Nobody forced you to. In fact, Jason had told you not to. I heard him. You should have known Jeff couldn't jump that gate."

"He could have, but something was wrong with him."

"He's getting old."

"No, there was something else. He wasn't acting right."

"If you noticed, why did you go riding? And in your robe?"

"I was standing by my window when I saw Jason coming up the lane from the stable. He waved and called that Jeff needed some exercise. I was so excited I just flew out of my room without waiting to change, afraid Jason would change his mind and say I couldn't go. I shouldn't have trusted him, though. He changes his mind so quickly!"

He's not the only one, I thought. I wanted to ask her more questions, to find out how she got out when I'd left the door locked, but she suddenly asked, "Did you bring me a surprise like you promised?"

"Yes." I'd been holding the package out of sight, and presented it to her.

"What is it?"

"Something pretty and feminine to go with all your new clothes." I held it close to her left hand so she could hold it for a moment and look at the lovely wrapping.

Instead of admiring it, she struck it away, and it went flying out of my hand. I picked it up and put it on the table by her bed. "We can open it later when you're in a better mood for gifts," I said, keeping the irritation out of my voice. Hadn't I learned anything about dealing with her? "What would you like for breakfast?"

"Where's Hattie? She knows what I like and can bring it up here."

"Jason gave her the day off. She's very upset about you and he thought she needed to rest. You know Hattie's a person with feelings, right?" *Like me*, I wanted to add.

"I want her back here, right now," Marian insisted, apparently oblivious to the idea that Hattie might have needs of her own. "Send her upstairs the minute she gets back. I won't have Jason taking her away. She's my protection."

"From what?"

"From Jason and from you too. Hattie is the only one who really cares about me and looks after me."

"I try to do that too, but you make it really hard sometimes."

"Sometimes I think you're on my side and pretend you're my younger sister."

"I thought you pretended I'm your mother." I regretted saying it immediately, but fortunately Marian didn't seem to have noticed.

"Most of the time you don't fool me. I know you're working for Jason."

"I'm working for both of you." *And I do mean work*, I thought.

"I mean working *for him*, against me."

"Marian, I'm not. Is there anything I can do or say to show you that I care about you?"

"I'll think it over," she said like an aggrieved child.

"You could open your gift," I suggested.

"You open it for me."

I removed the ribbon bow and took off the wrapping, folding it carefully as I'd been taught as a child and laying it aside. I lifted the box lid, displaying the lavender linen fabric and the bottle of cologne, and set it where she could see it.

Her face twisted in anger. With her left hand she plucked out the bottle and tossed it awkwardly across the room. It shattered, filling the air with an oppressively strong smell of lilac. "You did this deliberately, didn't you?" she demanded. "How did you know?"

"Know what?" I was shocked and puzzled at her reaction.

"That was my mother's favorite color, and she sprayed herself with lilac scent just before she left, the day she died. Who told you? Jason? Or Hattie? Oh my God, what if Hattie is against me now too?!"

"I'm so sorry. I didn't know anything about it." I almost said that I hadn't known how her mother died until Adam told me, after I'd made the purchases, but I stopped myself just in time. The less I said the better. "I thought lavender would be a good color on you, and I remembered a faint hint of lilac when you offered me your mother's clothes. And nobody is against you!"

"I don't believe you. Get Hattie here to clean it up. I can't stand smelling it."

I tried to put my hand on her left arm, her but she shook it off. "Get out! Go down and sit on the patio and enjoy being young and free, and maybe Jason will come out and play with you."

I bit my tongue to hold back what I longed to say. The mood she was in, no denial would change her accusation. "I'll clean it up," I said. "It was my mistake in buying it."

"Do what you like." She turned away from me.

When I returned with spray cleaner and a sponge, she asked as I opened the windows, "You didn't know my mother, did you, Kate?"

"No. You said she died many years ago."

"She did. You didn't even know my father. Has Hattie talked to you about my mother?"

"Hattie doesn't talk to me about anything."

We both jumped at the sound of a gunshot.

"What was that?" Marian demanded. "It was a shot, wasn't it? Jason has shot Jeff."

"You don't know that."

"I do! Jason shot my horse. He's trying to destroy me and everything I love."

Another shot rang out.

"He missed the first time. Go stop him! Maybe Jeff's still alive. Go save him, Kate!" she begged.

In the sudden silence I said, "He must have hit the second time, but I'll go and see." In my mind I was hoping it wasn't what Marian thought it was and simultaneously cursing Jason for being so callous if Marian was right. When he said he'd have Jeff put down, I was picturing a vet's office and euthanasia, not a gunshot. Why would he do something so brutal, especially where Marian could hear it?

Marian began to cry, sobbing like a child. "Jeff was the only thing left of my life before except Hattie, and now he's gone." Her voice dropped to a whisper and she gripped my shoulder with her left hand. "Tell Hattie to be careful, Kate. And you're important to me, so he may try to destroy you next."

"I'll be careful," I said, trying to placate her and calm her.

"You're not taking me seriously. Promise me that if something worse happens to me, if I die, that you'll leave immediately."

"I promise. You're the reason I'm here."

She changed the subject again. "Poor Jeff! But he was injured, wasn't he? Maybe he was suffering and Jason wanted to put him out of his pain. Do you think it could have been that?"

"I went by the stable after your accident, and Jeff was badly cut. Even if he'd recovered, I doubt if you could have ridden him again."

"Poor Jeff. Maybe it's better he's dead."

"You can get another horse as soon as you're well."

"No," she sighed. "I have nothing left to live for."

"You have a lot: Jason and Hattie and Nate and Marbury Hill. And Adam. You're intelligent and you have a comfortable home. Most people in the world would envy you."

"Well, the world is full of fools."

"I'll see if I can find Nate. Do you want breakfast now, or shall I let you sleep?"

She turned to me with eyes devoid of any expression. She was in shock, mourning her beloved horse. I might as well have not been there. Then she said in a faraway voice, "Do my hair the way you did it once that Jason liked."

I reached for the brush and began to arrange her hair.

"Jason used to brush my hair. He used to do all sorts of nice things for me, but that was then."

I brushed until her eyes began to droop. I thought she was asleep, and quickly pinned up her hair. I was tiptoeing out when she said softly, "Goodbye, Kate. Thank you."

Hattie came back just before noon, refusing my offer of help so she could have an entire day off. "Naw, Miss Marian gets upset when I'm gone too long. Did she ask for me?"

"Yes. She was upset that you weren't there, but you had every right to take some time for yourself—"

"Child, looking after her is my responsibility and always has been. I comforted her when her mother run off and got killed, and again when her father died. The only time I didn't look out for her was when she went off on that ship and met *him*."

"She's my responsibility too, Hattie," I said, though I wasn't sure she heard me.

As she started up the stairs, she turned to ask, "He lock her in again?" I nodded and handed her the keys.

She came back shortly and headed for the kitchen. While Jason and I had lunch, she took a tray up to Marian.

We ate silently, like two strangers forced to share a table. Tension shimmered in the air between us. Finally he pushed back his plate and said, "All right, out with it. You're clearly angry at me for something."

"Why did you shoot Jeff this morning?"

"It had to be done."

"Not where Marian could hear. It was cruel. Don't vets…"

He cut me off. "You know, I could do without everyone second-guessing me at every turn. I'm used to it from Marian and Hattie, but I thought you might give me a break, if only because I'm the one paying you."

I felt my face go hot with humiliation at his rebuke, and I had to swallow a time or two before I could trust that my voice would be steady. "I apologize for overstepping my authority, Mr. Ashby, I'll go up and see about Mrs. Ashby." I stood to go.

He reached out to stop me. "I'm sorry. I'm upset and have a lot on my mind. I shouldn't have spoken so sharply. You're not just an employee here, and you know it."

What am I? I almost asked, but the look in his eyes silenced me. Instead, I moved away, to the French doors that were open to the sunlight.

"Stay and have a brandy."

"At lunch?"

"I'm having one. Join me."

"All right." I tried to scan the newspaper, but it was difficult to care about national news when so much was whirling about me. I felt as if I'd been living in a foreign country.

He poured me a brandy and put on "Rites of Spring." "It's appropriate for today," he said. "It's actually a perfect day outside."

"Perfect for what?"

"For anything. We could go riding."

I winced at the idea. "I wouldn't feel right about riding."

He went to stand by the French window, his profile outlined by the sunlight. Suddenly he stiffened. "What was that?"

"What?"

"I thought I heard something in Marian's room." He set down his brandy glass. "I'll go check. Noises from her room make me skittish. Is her room still locked?"

"Yes. I gave you back the key after Hattie took her lunch up."

"So you did," he said, patting his pocket as he went out.

I sipped my brandy and tried to read the newspaper, but couldn't keep my mind on it. I was listening for Jason, waiting for him to come back and say he'd been mistaken.

Then I heard Marian scream, "Keep back!"

"Don't move, Marian!" he called out.

I ran out onto the patio and looked up at Marian's window. It stood open and I could make out the pink blur of her nightgown. "Don't come near me! Leave me alone!" she screamed. "*Help!*"

I ducked back inside and ran for the stairs. Before I was halfway up I heard a high, piercing scream that ended in a sickening thud. I knew before I went back to the patio what I'd find there.

Marian lay like a fallen pink flower, crushed on the white cross she'd painted. Her bandaged wrist jutted at a grotesque angle, as though she'd thrust out a hand to break her fall. Her eyes, like the glass eyes of a china doll, stared unseeing. I couldn't make myself go to her; I knew she was dead and there was nothing I could do for her.

I looked up at her window. White bed sheets fluttered against the wall. Where had she gotten them, and how had she knotted them together? She must have been planning this for days, before her injury, and hidden them from me. But she must have known she couldn't hold on to make her way down with one wrist broken. Why had she tried anything so futile? But then, why did she do a lot of things? My questions went on and on, and I kept hearing Marian's voice talking about Varina: "She was dead and they couldn't ask her."

I kept hearing Marian's scream over and over. Then I realized it wasn't Marian's; it was mine. I screamed until Jason grabbed and shook me. I hadn't heard him come down. I hadn't heard anything but the screams.

Hattie was the first to go to Marian. She dropped to her knees on the stones and bowed her head. As she softly rocked back and forth, looking into Marian's sightless eyes, she moaned over and over, "Poor child, poor child…"

I couldn't move. In the background I heard Jason saying into the phone, "Dr. Gordon, we need you and the coroner. We've had another accident and… I think my wife is dead."

Chapter 14

Officials came—Dr. Gordon, the county coroner, and the sheriff—and took over. They measured, drew chalk marks and wrote in notebooks. They made Marian's death official, but not real. She'd talked so much about her death, but it always seemed like a petty revenge fantasy. Now it had happened and yet it seemed more unreal than ever. I half expected her to look up from the patio and cry, "Fooled you!"

Jason described going up to Marian's room, seeing her at the window trying to climb out. "I ran forward to stop her, but…" He paused, swept his hands across his eyes. "I failed."

"Did she fall or jump?" the sheriff asked. "Or did you push her, Mr. Ashby?"

"Of course I didn't push her! I think she fell. She might have been trying to climb down on the bed sheets."

"And why would she be climbing out of her own bedroom? Why didn't she just walk down the stairs?"

"I shot her horse this morning. It was injured. She heard it and was upset. She may have been trying to go to the stable to see if Jeff was still alive," Jason admitted. "And I had her door locked for her own protection."

"Protection? From what?"

"From herself. She had attempted suicide before, but always in a half-hearted way—to get attention and sympathy, more than anything else. I think at the final moment she changed her mind and tried to get back into the window, but with her injury she couldn't hold on, and fell. If I'd been a few moments sooner, or if I'd crept up quietly and not startled her, she might still be alive."

"Hold on," the sheriff said. "You say she's attempted suicide before. Why wasn't my office notified?"

"Mental illness and attempted suicide are a personal matter," Dr. Gordon retorted. "It is of no concern to law enforcement until a death occurs."

"Well, one has occurred here, and we're trying to get to the bottom of it," the sheriff returned. He turned sharply to me. "You! Tell me what happened."

"Just what Mr. Ashby said," I responded, turning over in mind all Jason and the sheriff had just said. It all sounded sordid, like the fantasies Marian conjured up.

"Humor me. Tell me again. Where were you?"

"When?"

"When she died."

"Mr. Ashby and I were down here having a brandy after lunch," I began, realizing how that sounded, but there was no use evading and saying we were eating. The lunch things had been cleared away and our two glasses stood in mute testimony.

"You were drinking brandy together while Mrs. Ashby was upstairs alone?" the sheriff accused.

"She was heavily sedated because of her recent injury," Jason broke in. "Miss Flynn and I had been under a great deal of strain taking care of her, and we were having a small brandy to relax."

"I see," she sheriff said. "So why don't you let her go on and talk?"

"Mr. Ashby heard a noise from upstairs and ran to see about it."

"Did you hear anything?"

I hadn't heard anything, but I didn't want to cast any doubt on Jason. I nodded.

"What sort of noise?"

"A bump."

"Why didn't you go to investigate?"

"There was no need for both of us to go."

"But you are the employee, aren't you? Wouldn't it have been your job to go to her?"

"Yes, but Mr. Ashby acted more quickly than I. She's his—she was his wife and he was naturally concerned."

Jason met my eyes and smiled sadly. "Miss Flynn had already spent the morning with my wife."

The sheriff ignored him and asked me, "Did you actually see Mrs. Ashby fall?"

"No. I looked up and saw her at the window, and heard her calling. I was on my way up to help her when I heard her fall."

As he had done with Jason, he bored in on a part of what I had said. "She called out when her husband was in the room with her. Why do you think she did that?"

"I don't know."

"What did she actually say?"

"She called for help."

"Help in climbing down?"

"Possibly. She often talked of 'escaping' and to humor her I told her I'd help her escape when the time came. She fantasized about a lot of things," I concluded.

"So when you heard her call, what did you do?"

"I ran back inside and started upstairs. I was on the stairs when I heard her fall."

"So you don't actually know what happened?" He placed extra weight on the word "know" and his eyes seemed to bore into me, throwing doubt on what I said.

"No." Something was bothering me, some idea that didn't fit, but I couldn't say just what, so I pushed it to the back of my mind until I could think of it further.

"Do you think Mr. Ashby might have pushed his wife out that window?"

"Oh, no!" I burst out. "He loved her. He hired me to live here and protect her."

"And you failed." My heart sank, and I nodded. He'd put into words what I'd been thinking ever since that dreadful scream. I'd failed Marian and I'd be leaving Marbury Hill.

"I'm putting this down as an accidental death," the coroner announced. "I think we've done all we can here. We do have to take the body in for a simple autopsy, which is standard in cases when someone dies outside a hospital. We will of course be testing for drugs, especially as you said she was sedated, but we don't have a backlog at the crime lab, so you can go ahead with funeral arrangements, Mr. Ashby."

"I'll go along with your decision, doctor," the sheriff said to the coroner. "For now." He slapped his notebook shut and shoved into a pocket stretched tight against his ample abdomen. "We'll be on our way. I may have more questions later after the autopsy."

It wasn't until the officials had driven away with Marian's body and Jason came back into the library that I realized I'd been clenching my fingers so tightly that my nails had cut into my palm.

"So… that's that," Jason said grimly. "I have to go with Lucas to the cemetery to point out where the grave will be. Would you come with me?"

"Is the cemetery in town?"

"No, here on the plantation, near the bridle lane."

"Marian never mentioned it."

"She only showed it to me once and then never wanted to go near it again. I'd like some company, if you don't mind. This could get pretty rough."

We walked past the freshly planted flower beds, the neatly trimmed grass and the empty swimming pool, cleaned by Lucas and Nate, ready for painting and filling. Marian would never swim in that pool or see those flowers bloom. It was all wrong to be walking toward her gravesite on such a beautiful afternoon. Tragedy demanded dark nights and moss-covered walls, not the neat green and sun-drenched white of Marbury Hill. I turned at one point to look up at Marian's window. After taking photographs, the sheriff had removed the bed sheets. The wall looked as it always had, with no indication that a tragedy had just taken place.

We walked carefully apart, not speaking. Robins hopped along in front of us, trying to shoo us away from their nests then flying away. Down toward the river, frogs croaked. Marbury Hill was coming alive with springtime, and that seemed wrong, with Marian dead.

"Marian was never a happy person," Jason said, as if reading my thoughts.

"It wasn't your fault, Jason. You did what you could," I offered in consolation.

"I didn't say it was my fault," he shot back. "Nobody could have made her happy. But at least she was alive. I let her die."

I let his anger slide, as it was almost certainly motivated by guilt. "If you want to blame someone, blame me. I failed her too."

"But maybe I could have done more to make her happy," he went on. "I didn't tell her often enough that I loved her. She could be sweet sometimes, so full of life and excitement."

He was already focusing on the best parts of Marian. Similarly, I was remembering her loneliness rather than her mercurial mood changes and harsh accusations. And I felt some guilt and shame that Jason and I had shared music, food and drink, and thoughts that shut Marian out.

Everyone should be mourned for, and I was relieved to see Jason grieving. I hoped that when my time came, someone would remember the best parts of me.

A moss-covered brick wall enclosed the cemetery. A tangle of honeysuckle had knotted itself around the gate so that Jason had to take out a pocketknife and cut it loose before he pushed it open. Inside, new grass pushed up among the dried remains of last year's grass.

Like the exterior of the mansion, the cemetery had been neglected. A granite shaft thrust up in the center, its deep engraving almost filled in with lichen. I went closer and could make out "Captain Calvin Marbury, Sarah Wilson Marbury" and the dates of their births and deaths. There were no epitaphs, no phrases like "Beloved Wife," just names and numbers. Boxwood surrounded the monument and bordered the walks dividing the cemetery into sections. White narcissus, the old fashioned kind with single petals and yellow centers, once obviously planted between the graves, now sprang up with abandon everywhere. I smelled lilac, and saw one planted at the head of Marian's mother's grave.

Lucas and Nate came then with spades, and while Jason showed them the only space remaining—as if Captain Calvin Marbury had known just when the line would end—I moved among the tombstones, deciphering the history of the Marburys. They had been a patriotic family, but an unfortunate one. Some had fallen at Manassas, Gettysburg, San Juan Hill, Belleau Woods, Okinawa, Chosen. Babies had been born and died within a year. Varina's parents had died within a year of her death, perhaps of grief. Or guilt. There was the second Varina, who had lived well into Marian's lifetime. I turned to inquire of Jason and he answered without my asking: "She went berserk when her husband was thrown from his horse and killed a week after their marriage. She spent the next forty three years in a mental institution."

"I wish I could have made a difference for Marian," I said miserably.

"The only one who could have made a difference shaped Marian in the wrong way. Whenever Marian misbehaved as a child, Olivia would threaten, "I'll take you to live with Aunt Varina." It affected Marian long after Varina and Olivia were both dead."

I turned to Olivia's grave. I'd worn her clothing, smelled her cologne, heard how she'd died, sat in her favorite chair and now I stood before her final resting place. I broke a sprig of lilac, breathed in its fragrance, then flung it away as the scent reminded me of the last time I spoke to Marian.

As Lucas and Nate finished clearing the heavy growth atop the grave plot and began digging the grave, we turned back toward the mansion. It looked white and welcoming in the sunlight.

"What will you do now, Jason? It's all yours."

"I'm not sure. I'm still too shocked to make plans. When we first came here I hated the place and all it stood for. I felt like the illustrious ancestors were looking over my shoulder, disapproving of me. But now I think I'll stay on. Marbury Hill has cast a spell on me—or a curse."

"I understand. I felt the same… though not as much, of course," I said lamely.

"I wish I could ask you to stay, Kate, but I can't."

I was horrified to find that I was disappointed and even a bit hurt by his gentle rejection. Could I really want him to want me, when his wife was only hours dead? What kind of horrible person would do that?

He took my hand and I had a hard time meeting his eyes. "Perhaps after some time," was all he said, but I barely listened. What was I thinking? Adam was much better, safer, for me.

Adam! No one had called him. He might hear from someone in town who thought he already knew. I called him, and he said he'd be over soon.

I spent the afternoon packing, pulling garments off hangers and stuffing them into my suitcases heedless of wrinkles, in a frenzy to be gone. I made sure the little carved chest was just where I had left it in my closet. I must be sure to give it to Adam, one of the tasks I'd promised Marian I'd carry out, and the last I could fulfill. I borrowed Hattie's key and unlocked Olivia's room, replacing the borrowed parka and boots.

Word of Marian's death had spread, perhaps through the sheriff's office. Though no neighbors had come to visit in all the weeks I'd been at Marbury Hill, callers arrived all the next day with food, and a florist truck made the long drive to deliver a huge bouquet of white lilies. Jason wandered around, at odds, not knowing what to do. I took the keys and unlocked the big parlor and the music room and saw that Hattie had kept both shrines dusted. The lilies' fragrance overwhelmed the room. Who had sent them? There was no card. Jason came into the parlor and said bitterly, "So they finally arrived. I wanted them for her room when she got home from the hospital, lilies instead of lilac…." He turned and walked away.

The dining room table and the sideboard were loaded with food offerings: casseroles, cakes, pies, molded salads, home-baked breads and platters of fried chicken and ham biscuits. Hattie arranged and rearranged the refrigerator to hold the bounty, and still more came. "What we going do with all this, Miss Kate? Only three here to eat, five if you count me and Nate."

"Do you know anyone who could use the food? Maybe the farm workers' families?"

"I do know folks that would appreciate it. I'll take care of it." The look of approval that passed across her face and the tone of her voice told me she had stepped into the role of lady of the house. She was now the keeper of Marbury Hill, not Jason, and certainly not I.

Adam arrived just before dark and listened silently while Jason told him what had happened. I'd only said on the phone that Marian had died of a fall. After Jason finished, Adam looked to me for confirmation, and when I nodded, his mouth tightened for a moment. Then he said, "If you're going back to Richmond, I'll be glad to take you and help you get settled," he offered.

"There's no hurry—" Jason began.

Before he could say anything more, I cut in quickly. "Thank you, Adam. I accept."

When Hattie came in and saw him, her tears spilled over, and she sobbed against his shoulder. I realized hers were the first tears shed since the sheriff had left. Neither her husband, her cousin, nor I—who called her a friend—had cried for her.

Most of the callers had been older people who said they'd been friends of Marian's parents. Only one, a slim, well-dressed blonde, said she'd gone to college with Marian. It made me realize that I'd never asked where Marian went to school. We had to write an obituary with few facts to go on. She'd shared with me her dreams and fantasies, but no real information.

"Marian would have known me as Diana Ridgeway," the woman said to Jason. "I was several years behind her in school. I'm Diana Chase now. If there's anything I can do, please call me. I'm in the book. I've lost someone, and I know what you're going through." She glanced at me, clearly wondering what my position in the household would be. "I'm nearby at Oak Hill, staying with my mother." She laid a slim, manicured hand on Jason's arm and let it linger briefly; his eyes widened slightly and I felt a tiny jolt of jealousy so mortifying that I actually frowned a bit.

Just then Adam appeared at my side and walked me into the dining room. He seemed to have mercifully misread my frown because he said, "I know. She's not even being subtle about it. 'If there's anything I can do, please call me,'" he mimicked Diana's simpering delivery. Then his mouth tightened as he spat, "But he doesn't have to be so obviously flattered by it! Marian's body isn't even in the ground, and—" he stopped, as if realizing the physical truth of what he had just said. His shoulders deflated, and he sank into a dining room chair.

I knelt next to him and tried to put my arms around him, but he shrugged me off. "No," he muttered, clearing his throat as he stood, "no, I need to get back out there and at least stand next to him so someone is actually representing Marian."

"I could do that for you," I offered, as a devious part of my brain whispered, *That way I could keep an eye on Jason.* I tried to ignore it.

"Why would you do that? You're not family." He turned and left the room, as I sat down in the chair he had vacated.

My tears came then, spilling down my face in grief, loss and humiliation. His voice had no malice when he said it, just confusion, and it was certainly true that I wasn't family, but I felt that with those three words he'd cut me off from Marian, Jason, Marbury Hill and him. I found a napkin to blot my tears and stayed in the dining room, consolidating platters of appetizers and cookies, trying to make myself appear useful if anyone came in for food. Before long, Hattie came in, muttering "Miss Marian not even cold before that woman circling around him like a buzzard. She deserve him. He was no good for Miss Marian nor any other woman."

She and Adam were always in agreement, while I was usually defending Jason, but this time I was angry at him. Was he actually flattered at Diana Chase's overtures? Couldn't he see how it looked to have someone flirting with him at his wife's wake? *And was she his type, rather than I? Did he approach me because he wanted me, or just because I was convenient?* that devious voice asked.

When the last guests had gone and I heard Jason close the front door and head for the library, I started to go upstairs, intending to avoid both him and Adam. I couldn't count on myself not to start crying again.

Then I heard Adam's voice from the library, sounding angry. I tiptoed closer to the library door, staying close to the wall. I could hear him demand, "...at least tell me the truth now. There's nobody here to use as a distraction; Kate's not here to take your side; even Hattie's gone to bed."

"Honestly, Adam, I have no idea what you're talking about." Jason's voice sounded weary, and I couldn't blame him. *Wait,* I caught myself, *there I go taking his side. But he's bereaved; shouldn't that count for something?*

"The truth about Marian's death." The silence after Adam's last word felt especially deep, and Jason didn't rush to fill it.

After a moment, he said in that same weary tone, "Marian fell from her window."

"I thought you said she jumped," Adam cut in, a strain to his voice.

"I wasn't sure how she exited the window, but I know she did it by herself," Jason's voice now had an edge to match Adam's. "Kate corroborated the facts, and she's not lying."

"I don't think she'd deliberately lie, even for you," Adam said. "But I do think you brought her here as a patsy, to provide you a handy alibi. You know, I've gotta hand it to you: it must have taken some close planning to have things work out so well. Nice work, Jason."

He stalked out of the library so quickly I couldn't hide or escape. We looked at each other, startled; we both opened our mouths to say something, but no words came out. I shrugged and shook my head as Adam sighed and stalked upstairs.

I stayed just outside the library door, looking in at Jason like a child at a store window. He went to the liquor cabinet, poured himself a brandy and lifted the glass as if offering a toast to an unseen companion. He smiled, swirled the brandy, and then sipped it with slow obvious enjoyment. He didn't look my way, but I kept watching him, storing up images for the future when I wouldn't be able to see him.

Finally I tore myself away and crept up to my room. I looked out the window into the darkness, needing no light to see Marian cantering down the lane on Jeff, smearing paint on the lawn furniture and painting her cross on the flagstones. I could hear her commanding me to brush her hair, or telling me some fairytale about Jason or her mother. The house and my mind were too full of memories.

I went to the closet for Marian's little chest I was to give Adam. I ran my hand over the smooth lacquered surface, my fingers lingering at the clasp. I had the key. I could unlock it and satisfy my curiosity. No one would ever know. But she hadn't allowed me to see the contents in all the times she'd shown it to me or talked about it. She'd made me promise to give it to Adam, and I'd keep that promise. Though I was as convinced as Jason was that the box contained only childhood mementos, I'd treat it as something precious.

I heard Jason come upstairs, walking deliberately, making no effort to muffle his footsteps. He paused before my door and tapped lightly. I stood very still, hoping he'd think I was asleep. So often he'd knocked on my door to tell me Marian needed something, but that was over. I'd failed her when she needed me. But could I have helped then? Could I have ever helped her, from the first?

I didn't know what he wanted, and I dared not ask. When I didn't answer or open the door, Jason went on to his room and I heard the door close with finality.

Chapter 15

Marian had cautioned me not to let Jason know about the box, so I had to find a way to get it to Adam secretly. He'd be taking me to Richmond, but in the melee of the funeral and leave-taking, it might be forgotten. I took it downstairs, pausing to listen for anyone moving about and eased open the front door. A full moon was rising, and by its silvery light I saw Adam's pickup parked to the left of the house. I put the little chest behind the driver's seat and put his briefcase atop it. If I forgot to mention it to him in the confusion of the next few days, he'd find it sometime.

The night was almost unbearably beautiful. I stood for a moment leaning against the dew-chilled pickup, tears streaming down my face. I couldn't have said exactly why I was crying—for Marian, for myself or for the poignancy of life itself. The moonlight made a chiaroscuro of the mansion, its walls and columns ghostly white against the darkness of trees. I looked long, storing up memories to nourish me in the months to come.

Finally I made my way back inside, and as I eased closed the heavy front door, I heard a sound above me of something moving. *It's probably nothing. A house this old is bound to shift and sigh in the night like a sleeping person,* I thought, and started lightly up the steps. Then I heard a second sound, this time a definite click of a door lock. Someone was in Marian's room.

I went into my own room, locking the door behind me, and leaving the lights off. I went to the window, pulled back the curtains and looked across to Marian's room. The small darting light told me someone was moving about with a little flashlight. I thought of investigating, but whoever it was had more business there than I did. After all, I wasn't family.

I slept fitfully and awoke to bright sunlight. A glance at my watch told me it was already nearly eight. Even though I knew breakfast would be ready and getting cold, I took a little extra care with my appearance. I wanted to look nice for this last day here. When I was finally ready, my hair lay smooth and shiny, my makeup was perfect and my gray linen suit and print blouse brought out the blue in my eyes.

In the dining room Adam and Jason sat at opposite ends of the long table, silently drinking coffee and ignoring each other. A place had been set for me on the side, so I had to look from one to the other. The bounty of food from the night before had been stowed away or distributed by Hattie, so I didn't have to see any of it and be reminded of my embarrassment. I hoped Marian had left Hattie a substantial amount in her will; she'd earned every penny of it.

When Hattie set my breakfast plate before me she asked, "You leaving soon, Miss Kate?"

"Right after the funeral."

"You can stay longer if you need to, Kate. No one else needs your room. And I could use your help with all the business and notes that are bound to arrive," Jason said.

"No, I have to get my life back on track, and the sooner I go, the better."

"I'll be ready to leave as soon as the funeral is over," Adam said.

"I can take you," Jason offered.

"I'm going anyway," Adam said, "so it's no bother."

All of their statements were addressed to me, as they apparently weren't speaking to each other. Under different circumstances I might have laughed, but as it was I felt trapped between them. I just wanted the day to be over. "Then it's settled," I announced. "I'm going with Adam."

We were still at the table when Diana Chase arrived, elegantly clothed in a black dress, black sandals and black-toned hose. I suddenly felt like I was dressed for a business meeting by comparison. She laid a hand on Jason's shoulder and bent to kiss him lightly on both cheeks. "I know the funeral isn't until ten thirty, but I thought I might be helpful beforehand." Then, as if she'd just noticed Adam and me, she said brightly, "Hello again, Adam, and good morning, Miss … Flynn," she finished triumphantly, as if it had been an effort to remember my name.

She sat down opposite me and turned to Jason. "There will be notes to write for the food and flowers, and dishes to return, and you won't have Miss Flynn any more to help out."

This was awkward, and I didn't want to stick around for another confrontation between Jason and Adam. "If you'll excuse me, I still have some packing to do." As I left the dining room I heard Adam say behind me, "And I'd better get my stuff together too, so we can leave soon after the funeral."

He caught up with me on the stairs. "Let me know when you're ready for me to bring down your bags. I may need to rearrange a few things."

"I put something in your truck last night, a little carved box Marian made me promise to give you. I wasn't sure I'd see you in private today, and she didn't want Jason to know you have it. Come into my room and I'll give you the key."

He stood just inside my door and when I handed him the key, he took my hand and said, "Just a few more hours, and you can put all this behind you. I know you don't like the Chase woman, but I'm actually glad she showed up. She'll keep Jason occupied so he won't have a chance to be alone with you." He gave my hand a squeeze and went back down the stairs, leaving me to wonder what he'd meant by that last part. At some point, I'd have to talk with him about how jealousy is never a good look.

The morning passed in a blur. I remember little except the growing warmth of the day and the oppressive smell of flowers, especially the lilacs on Olivia's grave. Adam and Jason stood together, the only family. After the closing prayers we turned back toward the house, and I could hear clods of dirt being shoveled onto Marian's coffin. I said my goodbyes to Hattie, Nate and Lucas, then Adam took my arm and led me toward his pickup, where he'd stowed my remaining luggage.

As Adam closed the door, Jason strode rapidly toward us. "Kate, wait! I haven't had a chance to tell you goodbye."

I reached my hands to him through the open window of the pickup.

"I hope..." I began, but couldn't find the right words to say because I wasn't sure what I hoped for Jason. Adam made the point moot as he suddenly drove away with a spurt of gravel, leaving Jason standing alone. I looked back at him until we passed through the stone gateposts and he was lost to my view.

As we drove between the sentinel rows of dark cedars, I turned for a last look at Marbury Hill, though I'd promised myself I wouldn't.

I thought Adam hadn't noticed me looking until he gently said, "Remember what happened to Lot's wife, Kate. Don't look back. It's over." He paused at the highway, shifted gears and pulled onto the winding blacktop road.

As we crossed the bridge, I remembered the first time we'd crossed it. Then everything had been new to me, before I'd formed impressions. Now those impressions were fading, mile after mile. "I wish I could go back and be nicer to Marian, more understanding."

"Do you really think that could have changed anything? One way or another, Marian was bound to have some kind of 'tragic accident' eventually," he said darkly.

"Do you really think Jason killed her?"

"Time will tell. Or maybe it won't. We may never know for sure."

I couldn't really argue with that, so I tried to think of something else to talk about. What had we talked of when we had lunch together and dinner at his cabin? I tried to conjure up the images of that evening, of soaring in the swing, of standing by the fire, of his mouth on mine. I turned to study his profile. Movie producers would probably call him "ruggedly handsome," with his strong features and thick wavy hair, but to me he just looked strong, steady and real. I longed to touch him, to reassure myself that out in the world beyond Marbury Hill people like him had jobs, shopped, fell in love, cared for their families.

"Something wrong?"

"No. Why?"

"I can always feel when someone is staring at me. Have I developed some hideous scar or flaw?"

"Well, there is that third nostril, but I wasn't gonna say anything." He and I chuckled.

Several miles passed in silence before I asked, "Where are we going?"

"Richmond, like I said."

"Yes, but where in Richmond? I need to figure out where I can stay. When I got the job, I gave up my apartment and put my belongings in storage. I didn't think I'd be back so soon."

"Well, you don't have to stay in Richmond, but it's not a bad city. A bit stuffy, not as fast-paced as New York or California, and the weather in summer is almost unbearable, but you know all that. The cost of living is low, and that can help. I hope you were well compensated by you-know-who."

"I opened a bank account with my check," I said. "I can draw that out. I think I'll have enough to last me a few months."

"So then you won't be a burden on me if I let you stay at my apartment in town until you get settled."

"What makes you think I want to stay with you?"

"For one thing, I won't charge you rent. For another, it can be strictly platonic. I don't think we should get involved with each other right now."

"All right, thank you. I accept, at least for tonight. Tomorrow I'll see about finding a place of my own." I was a bit disappointed to hear him rule out a relationship with me, but he had a point about the timing.

Some of my disappointment must have shown on my face, because he said, "Look, no offense, but this has been a really… weird time for both of us, and I want to wait until you've gotten completely free of Marbury Hill and all of its occupants."

"What do you mean?"

"I mean Jason," he said gently. I started to protest, but he continued, "I know the kind of effect he has on women; I've seen it over and over again, starting with Marian. You might have thought he had some kind of feelings for you, but I promise you: now that you've served your purpose, he's done with you. And it looks like he's already moving on to that lacquered blonde anyway."

I was so stunned I couldn't answer, but he wasn't finished. "Let's be honest here: you're not rich enough for him. I just want you to know exactly where you stand. Ask yourself what you have to offer him that he can't find in half a dozen other women. He doesn't want companionship or romance; he wants money and power. You don't have either. But Ms. Chase has both. Whatever you think he might have felt for you, there was never really anything there."

He was looking steadily at me, and I felt the sincerity of how much he believed what he was saying, even as I wasn't thrilled with him for spelling it out quite so brutally. But was he actually right, or had his viewpoint been irrevocably warped by his belief that Jason might have killed his cousin?

As if sensing that I was thinking about Marian, he shifted his mood in a way that recalled her: "Hey, want a burger? They've got good ones here," he said, exiting the interstate.

By the time we reached Richmond, the sun was slanting low across the James River, throwing bright shadows on the water. We entered the city by way of the Powhite Parkway, and from there I was lost. Nothing looked as I'd remembered it. I felt as if I'd been away years, not months. Adam made several turns before pulling into the parking lot of a brick high-rise building.

"This is home," he said. "Let's take your things up."

I don't know what I expected his apartment to be like, but compared with his cabin it was austere. He switched on the light, dropped my suitcases by the door and said, "It's not much compared to the elegant appointments of Marbury Hill, but I think you can make do here for a night or two."

It was so impersonal, so different from his cabin or Marian's house. The furniture looked as if he might have ordered it by phone as a package deal: a sofa, two matching chairs and a glass-topped coffee table. Beyond half-empty bookshelves was a tiny kitchen that nonetheless had granite countertops and stainless steel appliances. Two high stools served as seating for the kitchen. He had done nothing to relieve the bare white walls, and the drapes had undoubtedly come with the apartment.

He grinned at my discomfiture. "You don't have to say it, Kate. I know what you're thinking: How does he stand living here? Usually, I don't. I go home to the cabin most weekends, and I travel a lot. When I'm in the Richmond office I get to work and stay late, so this is more like a motel than a home. One of these days I'll make enough to retire to the farm, or I'll just say the hell with it and move there anyway."

He led the way into his equally sparse bedroom. "Bathroom's through there if you need to freshen up. What would you like to drink?"

"Anything cold." My hair clung in damp tendrils to my forehead. His apartment, closed up for several days, was warm and stuffy.

When I came back into the living room, the air conditioner was whirring valiantly, and Adam was stirring a pitcher of daiquiris. He poured two stemmed glasses full and handed one to me. It's never been my favorite drink, but it was cold, and at that moment, delicious.

"What about some supper?" he asked. "We had a big breakfast, but I snatched you away before you could eat the food offerings after the funeral, and all you've had since was the burger."

"Though you were right; it was a pretty good one," I added.

He flung open the refrigerator door and peered in. "I might manage an omelet or scrambled eggs and bacon, but not much else. It'll be a letdown from dining at Marbury Hill."

"I've made do with bacon and eggs for supper when I was too tired to cook. I wasn't loaded before I went to Marbury Hill."

"If you'd rather, we can go out. I know of several good places near here."

"I'm too tired to go out. Pork and beans from a can actually sound much better than going to a nice place right now."

"Suits me," he said, and set about preparing our simple supper. We perched on the high stools and I forked down my food without noticing what it tasted like. I might as well have been eating the Styrofoam carton as the food itself. After the tension of the past days and weeks, I was deflating.

"I can see my culinary skills are wasted on you tonight, so I won't even try my collection of fine wines," he said sardonically. "You're ready to turn in, aren't you? Your eyes are about closed."

"I'm about ready to collapse." I slid off the stool but stood beside it for support. I looked out the window not across to Marian's window, but to a view of downtown Richmond, modern and glittering with lights.

Together we opened the sofa bed and made it up. I felt demure and sisterly, not at all sexy, in my pajamas and long robe. The air conditioner had cooled off the apartment, and I was actually chilly. He sat down beside me and began massaging my back and neck, his fingers gently kneading my tight muscles. "We need to do something to relax you," he said.

"Tomorrow," I returned sleepily.

He held me close for a moment. "Tomorrow we can do a lot of things. You've turned a page in your life. Or maybe you've reached the end of a book and closed it. Tomorrow you can start thinking about what book would be right for you now." He kissed my forehead. "Good night, Kate. Sleep well. You're safe here." He got up and started toward the bedroom, then turned back to say, "I'll be up at seven. If you're still asleep I'll try to tiptoe around and not disturb you."

"Seven's fine. Good night, Adam."

The door closed behind him. I got up and took off my robe, folding it and laying it across the sofa arm. I switched off the floor lamp and in the semi-darkness I could see a bit of the lighted city. I realized that several hours had passed since I'd thought of Marian or worried about what might be happening to her. For months my world had revolved around what she might do or say or need, and now I could think of myself only. Perhaps I could cope after all. If forgetting her for a few hours on the day of her funeral was this easy, then in time it might all start to fade from my memory.

Chapter 16

The next day, I combed through Craigslist until I found an apartment on the top floor of a Victorian house on Monument Avenue. The ceilings were ornamented with plaster medallions, the floors and doors were dark, and the ancient bathtub had claw feet. From the tall windows I could look down on flower sellers, strolling lovers, mothers with strollers and people walking dogs past haughty statues of Confederate generals.

It was what I wanted, a little quaint, but different from Marbury Hill and from Adam's Spartan space. I hoped that might help me get a little psychological distance from all of them, that they hadn't become a part of my life, inseparable and unforgettable.

After I'd gotten the few pieces of my mother's furniture out of storage and settled in, I invited Adam over for supper.

"Charming," he said, leaning back easily on the rosewood sofa, filling it and making my new space look small. "Now it's time to get a job."

"I have money to last a few months before I have to start looking, and I hate the applying and interviews. Why would I want a job now?"

"Because you'll go crazy if you don't," he said bluntly. "You can't sit around here all day waiting for life to happen—or waiting to forget everything that just happened."

"I don't know… Just doing nothing for a while sounds pretty good." It sounded brilliant, in fact.

"Tell you what: I'll do what I can to help you get a job for the rest of this week. But after that, you're on your own."

"What, are you crossing me off your list?" To my own surprise, I felt a bit of panic. I'd come to depend on Adam, on his rough kindness and good humor. What would I do without him?

"My geographic list, at least. I told you, I have to go to eastern Africa on business. Can I bring you something? Maybe some tea or coffee or a gemstone? I don't buy animal parts, so forget any skins or tusks."

"I wouldn't want them anyway. How long will you be gone?"

"You sound as if you might miss me."

I wasn't sure if he was teasing and hesitated a moment too long before saying, "I might."

The moment passed and he said casually, "Never know on these trips. It's scheduled for two weeks, but it could stretch to a month or more if we run into problems." He set down his coffee cup and stood. "I'd better get going. Give me a call at the office tomorrow and I'll see what I can line up for you."

I nodded. "Thanks, but I'm not making any promises about getting a job immediately. I do appreciate the thought, though," I added softly, and gave him a hug and a brief goodbye kiss.

It turned out Adam was right about my going crazy without a job; the next week I started working as an office manager for a dentist's office, and Adam left for Nairobi.

Spring turned to summer, and life moved more languidly. I was determined to show Adam—and myself—that I wasn't waiting for life to happen. I made myself go to new parts of Richmond, exploring it as if it were completely new to me. I got in touch with old friends, and I went to church for the first time in almost a year.

Lunches with friends were often bittersweet. My friends from high school and college were already paired off, and seemed concerned that I wasn't yet. They fretted about mortgages, in-laws and the best days for conception, all of which sounded alien and unpleasant to me. They showed me photos on their phones of their men, all of whom seemed to have the same plaid button-down shirt, pleated khaki pants, haircut and "dad body." I mentally compared them to Jason and Adam and wondered what my friends saw in these bland men.

When I watched the news and there was any mention of violence anywhere in Africa, I thought about Adam, and wondered if he were in danger. He hadn't called, emailed or texted me since he left. Perhaps he had crossed me off his list.

Friends detected my lack of interest and their half-hearted "Let's get together sometime" meant I'd been crossed off their lists too.

So I walked, seeing my familiar home city with new vision. I saw the white of the Capitol against a deep blue sky, heard the swish of traffic along Broad Street, ate brunch alone at the Jefferson Hotel. On weekends I'd take a lunch and a paperback book to Byrd Park and throw crumbs at the ducks.

After he had been gone for 2 weeks, I began to receive postcards from Adam postmarked Cairo, Nairobi, Cape Town, Lagos, all bearing short, impersonal messages: "Keeping busy," "Nice beaches here", "You'd like this," and "Miss you." I decided not to read too much into it and just focus on enjoying my time alone.

That changed on a Saturday in July, when I ran into my ex, Harold, while visiting the Virginia Museum. I was about to enter the glass exhibition when I saw him coming out. I turned away, but not quickly enough. "Kate!" he exclaimed, just as if we'd parted as friends, on totally amicable terms. He touched my hand and I pulled it back as if I'd been burned.

"It's so great to see you," he said. "You look great! Hey, are you free tonight? Maybe we could have dinner! Or at least drinks?" he added, seeing my reluctance.

"Ah, no, I've got plans. Besides, I don't think Mary Lou would appreciate it."

"Oh, that's over. We just had nothing in common, you know?" *You both seemed to enjoy cheating*, I thought, but said nothing. "And she wasn't even my type. Not like you." He moved closer, and I was aware of his size, his blond Viking good looks, and the blue of his eyes that whispered of the decadence and debauchery behind their seeming innocence. "So, where are you living these days? Are you on Facebook? How can I get in touch with you?"

"You can't," I said with finality, and walked away. My phone number had stayed the same; if he'd wanted me, he could have called me a hundred times. As I passed the great bronze sculpture of the cracked earth on my way out, I wondered what I had ever seen in Harold that made me think he was relationship material. *Sure, he was good-looking, but that gets old after a few months*, I thought with a smile.

Suddenly, Jason's face came to my mind, and I felt a pang in my heart. Would I have gotten tired of Jason after a few months? Or, if Adam was right about him, would he have even wanted me to stick around once Diana Chase was available?

I thought about Jason for the rest of the day, then finally gave in and dialed the number for Marbury Hill. Hattie answered and when I heard her voice, I realized how much I had missed her kindness and down-to-earth perspective, how rare both of them had been at Marbury Hill. "Hattie, it's Kate Flynn. How are you?"

"We doing okay," she said with a lack of enthusiasm. "How 'bout you? You got a job?"

"Yes! I manage a dentist's office."

"That sounds fascinatin'," she said drolly and we laughed together.

"How's Nate?"

"That boy…" Her tone had turned sadder. "He ain't been the same since Miss

Marian passed. He's been keeping to himself a lot, and I don't think he's said more than three words in a row to anybody since that day."

"I'm sorry to hear that," I said with real feeling. Nate had struck me as a sweet, sensitive kid, and this might have been his first time being faced with the death of someone he knew. "Please tell him I said hi, if you think it might help." I paused, hoping my change of subject wouldn't be too abrupt. "So, is Mr. Ashby there?"

"No'm, he ain't. He out riding with Miz Chase. They go riding nearly every day."

I paused. "Really?"

"Mm-hmm. She didn't waste no time, did she?"

"I guess not." My throat constricted at the image of Diana Chase leaning toward Jason, laughing, touching him. It looked like Adam was right: Jason didn't need me, hadn't even thought of me.

"Should I tell Mr. Ashby you called?"

"Ah… no." I don't know what I had expected; maybe that Jason would tell me he missed me and make a date for us to have lunch. But the more I thought about it, the more silly and naïve it sounded. "It's good to hear your voice, though."

"You too, Miss Kate."

"Take care of yourself, Hattie, and I hope Nate feels better soon."

"Thank you, Miss Kate, I will."

Over the next few days I tried to put Jason out of my mind, and occasionally succeeded. Then I'd see a lean, dark-haired man in a crowd, and I'd start toward him only to be confronted by a stranger. Or I'd walk past a tobacco shop and catch the acidic fragrance of the pipe blend Jason smoked. Once I even saw a woman who reminded me of Marian, until she bent down and spoke to a child in a New Jersey accent.

Finally, Adam returned from Africa, although he didn't call me until he'd been home a few days. We had lunch together, then met again for coffee, and I started to I wonder if he didn't want to see me in the evening or on weekends. *Or perhaps he was just busy, like people often are when they get back from a long trip,* I reminded myself.

A couple of weeks after he returned, he called to invite me to the beach for the weekend. I was delighted.

"What should I bring? What are we going to do?" I asked.

"Same answer to both questions: as much or as little as you want. I thought we could leave early Saturday morning, have a nice lunch by the sea, tour around Norfolk if you want, take a harbor cruise, have a seafood dinner and spend the night at the coast. For Sunday, we could do a few more touristy things, maybe check out Colonial Williamsburg, and get back Sunday night. Or, we could just hop in the car, head southeast and see what happens. How does that sound?"

"Great!"

"Good. I'll pick you up at 7 on Saturday morning."

It turned out to be a perfect beach day, sunny and breezy. We'd spread our towels and anointed each other with sunscreen when I asked teasingly, "Why did it take you so long after you got back to invite me out here?"

"I wanted to wait for the perfect weekend," he said, but I couldn't tell if he was teasing too, or if I just wasn't that important to him.

I decided that it didn't matter, as long we were enjoying ourselves. We played in the waves like children, laughing and holding hands and then we lay close together while he told me about Africa: the mineral wealth of South Africa, the haunting beauty of Kenya, the poverty in too many places. I had little to tell him. My life seemed pale and empty compared to his.

We bought ice cream and postcards at a boardwalk shop that also sold stamps, then sat down at a nearby table. On the back of an image of the beach at sunset, I wrote to my sister, suggesting that we should see each other soon. I addressed a picture of the Norfolk Naval Base to Jason and wrote, "Ships and the sea remind me of Marian and all her stories. Hope you're doing well." Part of me wanted to say something about how I'd been reminded of him too, but I worried that it would seem ridiculous, especially now that "Miz Chase" was such a regular part of his life. I sent another card to Hattie, and one to my father and his wife.

"I wonder if people send all that many postcards anymore," Adam pondered.

"I loved getting your postcards from Africa and I kept them all. Why did you send those?"

He smiled. "To keep my memory alive until I got back."

"Well, it worked." I leaned up toward him and we softly kissed.

As we strolled up the beach hand in hand, I saw a post office box. "Here, I'll mail your cards right now," Adam volunteered. "Otherwise, you might not find them in your bag again until next winter."

I thanked him and handed over the cards. He jogged over to the box, pulled down the flap and hesitated before he dropped the cards in.

He walked back to me, clearly upset. "You wrote to Jason?"

"Yes. You obviously read the message, so you know it was nothing inappropriate," I said defensively.

He sighed and glanced at his watch. "You know, I think we can get back to Richmond by dinner time."

"I thought we were staying over."

"I've changed my mind."

The trip back seemed to take forever, which wasn't helped by the fact that neither of us spoke to each other. He seemed disappointed in me for contacting Jason, and I was every bit as disappointed in him for making a big deal out of a postcard that was cordial, at best. *But you wanted to say much more on that postcard,* I reminded myself, and felt a touch of guilt in addition to my annoyance at Adam.

When he stopped to let me off in front of my apartment, I didn't want to invite him in, and I knew he wouldn't come in even if I did invite him. He reached across to shake hands with me rather than kissing or even hugging me. "I think we could have had a good relationship, Kate," he said. "Call me once you've got Jason completely out of your mind. Or once he uses you and throws you away, just like I said he would."

He drove off, ensuring that he'd have the last word. I was too drained even to make a rude gesture to his truck as it departed.

Chapter 17

The next day, I got up early, cleaned my apartment to within an inch of its life and took some clothes that no longer fit to Goodwill. I decided to focus on creating a new life for myself, without Adam or Jason or any other reminders of that time.

Still, when I heard my phone ringing as I got home from work on Wednesday, my first thought was that maybe Adam had decided to see if we could give things another chance.

But it wasn't Adam who had called. "Kate! How are you?" Jason's voice sounded as warm and welcoming as it had my first day at Marbury Hill, and my heart caught in my throat.

"I'm fine," I managed. "How are you?"

"Oh, I'm getting by. I got your postcard today, and it reminded me of you," he said softly. "I don't think we ever had a chance to really get to know each other, what with everything going on, and I was thinking it would be nice to just spend some time with you, if that's all right."

"That sounds fine," I said, hoping my voice didn't sound too eager.

"What are your plans this weekend? Do you think you could come up on Saturday, maybe stay through to Sunday?"

"Sure!" I said, and cringed at the tone of my voice. If I was trying to play it cool, I was failing miserably.

"Excellent. You know what, I'll even come by and get you Saturday morning, say around eight."

I gave him my address and hung up, with a smile on my face that refused to fade for the next two days. I spent those days choosing outfits, packing and getting a quick tooth-whitening treatment from the dentist I worked for at a nice employee discount.

Adam sent me a text on Friday, a tentative "Hey. You okay?" *You can't even work up the nerve to talk to me on the phone*, I thought angrily. I texted back "Yeah - going to Marbury Hill tomorrow!" with a smiley face. I didn't check to see if he responded; I knew I'd get either silence or his usual pouty anger. And I figured I didn't need that negativity, not when I could look forward to seeing Jason again.

And yet, when the BMW pulled up on Saturday and I finally saw him for the first time in months, I didn't feel the rush of joy I had anticipated. Perhaps I had gotten my hopes too high and was expecting more than he could possibly deliver.

He walked toward me with his arms open. "Kate, I have missed you so much." I expected him to embrace me, but instead he reached for my hands, just like the first time he had welcomed me to Marbury Hill. After clasping my hands firmly, he dropped them, picked up my overnight bag and said, "Come on, let's go. I've planned so many things for us to do that I can hardly wait to get you home."

Home. The whole time I had lived with the Ashbys, I had never thought of their house as home. But perhaps that could change?

On the drive he talked about nothing but the house. "I think you're going to be pleasantly surprised. I can't wait for you to see all I've done. I've repaired the road, had the shrubs pruned and the bridle trail trimmed back. I got the whole house painted so it looks the way it always should have. I've even finally made a profit on the farm operations."

"That's wonderful, Jason! And you seem really happy." I wondered if Diana Chase had been responsible for so many changes, including Jason's happiness, but I realized that I didn't want to ask him or hear the answers. *None of that matters,* I told myself. *He's here with you and that's what you wanted.* I studied his profile, looking for changes since the last time I'd seen him. He turned and smiled at me, and everything felt right. No more worries or questions, I promised myself. Just enjoy being here with Jason.

The air shimmered with late summer haze, and roadsides were bright with goldenrod, purple ironweed and black-eyed Susans. Fields of tobacco had been harvested almost to the topmost leaves that hung dappled and ripe. Apple and pear trees hung heavy with fruit, and freshly cut hay perfumed the air. It was a wonderful time to be going to Marbury Hill, much better than when I'd first arrived on a cold snowy day.

We passed through town, past the train station and the inn where I'd dined with Adam. Then we were out in the country, heading down the steep hill toward the creek. I tried not to let my panic show as we hurtled toward the bridge, going much too fast. At the last minute Jason hit the brakes and the sports car clung miraculously to the rough surface of the bridge and slid across, leaving black marks. The air smelled of burned rubber as we began to climb up the hill.

130

My heart was pounding with fear and I laughed almost hysterically with relief. Jason joined me, his laughter much more relaxed. "You don't have to worry. I've crossed that bridge so many times I could do it in my sleep. You don't think I'd take a chance on hurting you now that I've gotten to see you again, do you?"

"I hope not." I breathed easier as we crested the hill and the road flattened out. I recognized some of the farms we passed, and then there was the driveway to Adam's cabin. I felt a momentary pang of regret at how things had turned out between us. I might have come to love him in different circumstances. And then my heart beat faster with anticipation, because we were almost there.

The first change I saw was a white board sign with elegant lettering, reading "Marbury Hill, 1779."

"That's a nice touch, isn't it? Diana says I should open the house for garden tours next spring. That will help me get accepted into the hunt."

The mention of Diana Chase had made my heart stop and sink a bit. I turned to stare at him. Did he and Diana have plans for the future, or was she just advising him in a friendly way? "I like the sign," I said. "I think Marian would have liked it too. It's such a shame she didn't get to see it." That last bit was added as a bit of petty revenge for talking about Diana; I wasn't proud of it, but it felt rather good.

"Let's not talk about Marian, Kate. We have to put the past behind us and enjoy the present."

The driveway was freshly paved and bordered on both sides by white board fences and beds of red petunias. "This all looks so good you could enter it in the garden tour right now," I said.

"Just wait. There's a lot more."

When we approached the stone fence, Jason pressed a button on a little rectangle clipped to the sun visor and the tall black iron gates swung open silently. The pull chains were no more. As we passed through, I caught my first glimpse of the house itself, gleaming white and magnificent in the sunlight. Wrought iron furniture was arranged invitingly in the shade of trees beside the house and on the front porch of the house itself, beside huge urns of red geraniums.

"It's beautiful, Jason. I wish—" I started to catch myself, then continued, because it was the truth. "I wish Marian could have seen it like this."

"I know," he said softly. "But I spent so much time and effort taking care of Marian that I was never able to give the house the attention it deserved." He parked in front of the garage and we walked to the portico. He opened the door and called out, "Hattie! Miss Flynn is here."

She appeared, more subdued than I remembered her being while Marian was alive. "Miss Kate," she said, "I hope you'll find everything okay here. I fixed up your room ready—the room you used to have when you stayed here."

"I'm sure everything is fine, Hattie. It's good to see you again." I moved toward her, ready for a tentative embrace, but she turned away.

"Yes'm," she murmured. "Lunch is ready whenever you want, Mr. Ashby."

I wondered what had caused Hattie to act so differently. Perhaps I had only imagined the warmth and fondness of our phone conversation.

"Twelve thirty," he said, picking up my bag. "I'll take this up for you, Kate." As we went upstairs I looked back to see Hattie watching us.

Jason closed the door to the Rose Bedroom behind us, dropped my bag and pulled me into his arms. "Kate, it's so good to have you here. You can't know how good it is." He brought his mouth down on mine, blotting out my doubts. I responded with joyful abandon. And then I pulled back. He and I might be legally free, but Marian's presence hung over the room, imprisoning me in memories of the past.

"What's wrong, Kate?"

I couldn't tell him what I was feeling. "Won't Hattie be suspicious of us staying up here so long?"

"You're right. We'll have all the time in the world to be alone later, after she's served dinner and gone home. Let me show you the rest of what I've done, and after lunch we can ride."

I paused on the steps. "Ride?"

"Yes, I keep horses and ride nearly every day, and I'm a much better rider than I used to be. You'll have to try out Ali, my latest purchase." He kept talking as he led me out onto the patio where red petunias spilled out of wooden boxes and a clump of white caladiums filled in a shady spot. The lawn sloped downward in terraces to the boxwood garden. The patio had been cleaned, so a stranger would never know where bloodstains and a white painted cross had been.

Involuntarily I looked up at what had been Marian's window. A disturbing memory nibbled at my consciousness, not clear enough to examine but too troubling to dismiss.

Jason put his arm around me as we passed the swimming pool, and I was reminded of walking with Adam on the beach.

Almost as if he were reading my thoughts, Jason asked, "Do you see much of Marian's cousin in Richmond?" As if he didn't know Adam's name.

"Adam? Yes. He helped me get settled when I first got back. I've got an apartment and a job now."

"Do you like the job enough to stay, or do you think you might give it up under the right circumstances?"

"I don't know. It's good enough for now. I needed something to get my mind off—things."

"Did you and he ever go out? I thought you were getting pretty close when you left."

"Oh, that's… that's not worth mentioning," I said, not wanting to talk about how Adam's jealousy of Jason had basically doomed any relationship we could have had. "What about your social life?"

He shrugged. "There's not much of it. I've had people over for dinner several times, and I go riding with the neighbors. It's still isolated here. I don't have the opportunities you have in Richmond."

"I guess I'm just not that interested in all those opportunities," I admitted, looking into Jason's eyes. He looked back into mine so intensely that I felt the need to break his hold, and blurted out, "Adam's been in Africa most of the summer."

"Oh! Where is he now?"

"He's back in Richmond. I haven't really seen him much lately."

"Does he know you're here?"

"No. Why do you ask?"

"Just wondering."

"You know, Adam was always asking me about you, and now you're asking me about him. What's with you two?"

Jason ignored my question. "Are you in love with him?"

"Does it matter? I mean, you took a while to call me, so I didn't get the impression you were pining after me."

"I tried to forget you, but when your card came it brought back all kinds of memories. Why did you write it?"

"To get your attention," I admitted. "I also called one time, but Hattie said you were out riding with Mrs. Chase."

His face flushed with color. "Hattie didn't tell me you'd called."

"I asked her not to. Don't be mad at her. We're here now and that's what matters."

He glanced at his watch. "It's only 10:30. How about a short ride before lunch? I want you to see the new horses, a matched pair of Arabians, Sultan and Ali."

"I still don't own riding boots. Can I ride like this?" I indicated my capri pants and sandals.

"The hunt club wouldn't approve, but you look fine to me."

At the stable he called, "Nate, bring out Sultan and Ali."

Nate stopped short when he saw me, blurted, "Miss Kate," and almost let go of the horse's halter.

"Hello, Nate. It's good to see you again."

He continued to stare at me, his eyes large and white.

"Here, let me have Sultan. I'll saddle him," Jason said. "I've learned to handle horses, Kate."

The horses were glossy black with flowing manes and tails. They snorted and shifted, impatient to run. I felt uneasy at riding either one. Jason finished saddling Sultan and helped me mount. I reached forward to stroke Sultan's silky coat, but he wasn't in a mood to be soothed. Jason let his hand rest on my hip for a moment and our eyes met again; my heart was already beating hard from my anxiety about the horses, and the heat of Jason's closeness suddenly felt searing. Then he mounted Ali and raced off down the lane.

I dug my heels into Sultan and at my slight signal he galloped toward Ali. Jason halted and waited for me. When I came abreast, he set an easy pace and I followed.

I'd just gotten accustomed to riding when we came out into a clearing … only to see Diana Chase mounted on her chestnut horse, sitting as if she were posing for a hunting magazine in jodhpurs, scarlet jacket and black boots and hat.

"So this is what you do when you tell me you'll be away," she said. "It's the little nursemaid, isn't it?"

"Diana," Jason said with irritation, "you shouldn't have come. You don't own me." I realized that I had heard him use the same tone with Marian.

"Not yet," she said and turned away.

Just then a small dog darted from the woods and she called, "No, Gypsy!"

It was too late. Sultan reared and I felt myself thrown through the air, then landing hard. My face hit the dirt but my foot was caught in the stirrup. I screamed and struggled to get free. I'd be dragged to death if Sultan ran. Jason stared at me without moving. I was about to give in to sheer panic when the saddle finally slid off and hit the ground beside me. Sultan hesitated, and I was able to pull my foot free. I lay stunned and silent. My silly sandals had saved me. If I'd had on riding boots, my foot would have been trapped.

Jason grabbed Sultan's rein and called, "Diana, can you take care of the horses?" but she had gone, impervious to my fall. Holding both reins, Jason bent to ask, "Are you all right, honey?" *He had called Marian that, too*, I thought.

I couldn't speak. I was shaking and sobbing, more from relief and fear than from pain, though the side of my face was scraped raw, and I could feel blood trickling down my neck.

Jason picked up the saddle and threw it onto Sultan, but the strap that held it into place was broken. "Shoddy stuff," he said. "I just bought this. What if you'd tried to jump a hurdle? Thank God that didn't happen. This was bad enough. The strap breaking may actually have saved you. Can you ride back? I'll take Sultan and you can ride Ali."

I was in no hurry to get back onto a horse, but Jason boosted me up so quickly I could barely protest. "Are you all right, Kate?"

"Yes, but I probably need a tetanus shot."

"Of course. We'll get you to the Emergency Room so they can check you out as well."

Jason sat with me while the doctor examined me and gave me the tetanus shot. "You're probably going to be sore tomorrow, but you don't have any broken bones, so I'm writing you a prescription for infection and another for pain. If you have any swelling or dizziness, come back and we'll admit you and run tests."

Jason paid the ER bill, then we drove a few blocks to the local shops. "While you're getting the prescriptions filled, I'll go across to the hardware store and pick up another cinch strap," Jason said.

I entered the pharmacy, where I had purchased makeup and toiletries for Marian just a few months earlier. When the pharmacist handed me the prescriptions, he looked startled and then said, "I owe you an apology. I hope I haven't put you in danger."

"What do you mean?"

"Remember that little yellow pill you brought in for me to analyze, way back in the spring?"

For a moment I didn't remember. Then it came back in a flash: the pill I'd found on her pillow. I nodded.

"I hope you didn't take any more of them. I meant to call you, but a man answered the phone and said you didn't live there anymore and he didn't have a number to reach you. I wouldn't tell him what I wanted. Professional ethics."

Jason knew my number. Why hadn't he told me about the call? "I'm just back for a visit," I said. "What about the pill?"

"It's poison in large doses. Even one or two can cause vomiting and dizziness. Some people can tolerate them with no trouble, but I wouldn't take one for love nor money. We don't carry it. You must have bought it overseas."

Where had Jason gotten them? I didn't know. "Thank you so much," I said. "I'll try to find the rest of the pills and destroy them."

"Only thing to do."

I made my way back to the car and leaned against it, feeling sick, as if I'd swallowed one of the pills. Jason controlled the bottle. He could have been poisoning Marian just as she accused him, but maybe not intentionally. Were there still any of the pills left? I had to warn Jason to destroy them. But then he'd know I'd been suspicious enough of him to have the pills investigated.

"What's wrong?" Jason asked, opening the car door for me. "You look sick. Want me to take you back to the ER?"

"No. I'll be all right."

By the time we got back to the house, I felt calmer, but still shaky. "I should have taken you back," Jason said. "At least come into the library and rest for a while. Don't try to make it upstairs." He guided me into the library, his hand warm around my waist, the fragrance of his pipe lingering in the air to bring back memories. I wanted to believe that this was all a misunderstanding, that he'd never hurt Marian or me, certainly not intentionally.

"Sit down and let me get you a glass of water and something to relax you."

I watched as he unlocked the desk and took out the pill bottle. He shook one out and handed it to me. It was the same kind he'd had me give Marian, the kind the pharmacist had just told me to get rid of. "No, Jason, it turns out those pills are dangerous."

His eyes met mine with an enigmatic expression. Then he laughed. "So suspicious! Look, I'll take one to show you they're okay." He popped it into his mouth and swallowed it. "Don't blame me if I'm so relaxed I fall asleep over lunch. Now one for you."

"I probably shouldn't take it along with the prescriptions."

He shrugged. "Suit yourself. I'm not forcing anything on you."

Perhaps the pills weren't toxic at all. Or perhaps Jason had taken them before and built up an immunity to them. Or maybe Marian was susceptible and he wasn't. Hattie came to say lunch was ready and I pushed thoughts of the pills aside.

Hattie had prepared some of my favorite foods and I was lulled again by the luxury of Marbury Hill, the perfectly paired wine and Jason's amiable presence. I was caught off guard when he said, "Let's go finish our ride."

"What? No, I wouldn't feel safe."

"Don't you feel safe with me?"

"It's not you, it's the horse. I'd feel uneasy and the horse would sense it."

"All the more reason to go right back and face your fear. I promise you: you won't regret it. I was a really nervous rider, but I've gotten better because I keep getting back on that horse," he said, looking at me with warmth and encouragement.

And so I went with him to the stable for the second time that day. He paused to get the new leather strap and slapped it against his thigh as we walked.

Nate led Ali out already saddled. "Something's wrong with Sultan's saddle, Mr. Ashby."

"I know. The strap's broken. I have a new one right here. I'll only be a minute, Kate." He disappeared into the tack room.

"Miss Kate, look," Nate said quietly. He held out a leather strap. "It was cut."

I looked closely at the leather strap and saw that he was right. And we both knew who had most likely cut it: Jason.

Nate's eyes burned with guilt. He paused, then the words came out of him in a rush. "I don't want nothing bad to happen to you like happened to Miss Marian. He caused it."

"What do you mean?"

"That day when you went into town, Mr. Ashby came down here and saddled up Jeff. Then he went to tell Miss Marian to come and ride. He gave Jeff a shot of something with a big needle. To help with his joints, he said when he saw me watching. He said Miss Marian would be happy going riding. But she got kilt."

Marian had known. She'd told me Jeff had something wrong with him and I'd dismissed her fears. She'd been right about the pills too. I felt the world tilt around me as I realized how much danger I was in. For some reason I couldn't fathom, Jason had brought me here to kill me. But I wasn't Marian. I had my wits about me, and no broken bones. I was going to escape.

Chapter 18

With Nate's help, I leapt onto Ali's back and dug my heels into his sides, pulling his head around toward the house. If I could make it to the highway, I could flag down a car.

As I rode, I looked up at the house, its white walls gleaming in the sunlight. It was unbearably beautiful. I'd always carry that vision with me: the house set like a huge white gem in a sea of green. I glanced at Marian's window, at the bare white wall below it, and suddenly the missing piece of knowledge slipped into my mind, the realization hitting me so hard I almost fell off Ali's back.

The day Marian died, we'd been in the library, and after Jason went upstairs I heard her scream and looked up at her window. There had been no sheets fluttering there, only a blank white wall. I'd started for the stairs, heard her fall and run to the patio. I'd looked down at her body, not up, but when I did look up later, there were the sheets, coarse white sheets knotted into a rope. But they hadn't been there at first. And they were cotton. Marian always had satin. Jason, not Marian, had tied the sheets ahead of time and hung them out the window after he pushed her out. That was what my mind had refused to recognize for so long. I wouldn't let myself believe that Jason had killed Marian—and wanted to kill me.

"Kate!"

I glanced back over my shoulder and saw him running from the stable, waving and calling me. In that glimpse I imprinted his image on my heart. For one moment longer I let myself remember how it had felt to be in his arms. I almost turned Ali back toward him

Murderer! my mind screamed. *You can't be sure, even now,* my heart argued. My head and my heart agreed that loving him could have been marvelous, but it was over.

I leaned against Ali's neck, urging him faster, feeling his muscles strain as he plunged onward. We rounded the house and pounded along the white-graveled driveway. As we reached the stone fence, Ali leaped over it, taking me with him. He was magnificent, but he couldn't outrun a car, and behind me I heard the sound of an engine. At least Jason would have a short delay while the gate opened.

Ali pounded along the driveway, running as his instincts told him to, but unless a miracle occurred, his exertion wouldn't be enough to save me. Behind us I heard the racing engine and the blaring horn of Jason's car. Then, just as I reached the highway, I heard another car. I wheeled Ali around and began to wave, then realized that it was actually a truck—a truck I knew fairly well.

Adam slowed beside me, thrust open the door to the pickup and yelled, "Get in!"

I slid off Ali, giving his rump a slap. Adam turned the truck back toward town, and as I got in I saw Ali running back toward the stable. My heart stopped as I saw Jason bearing down on the horse. At the last possible moment he swerved aside.

"He didn't hit him," I said, my breath coming in shallow gasps.

Adam understood what I meant. "No, Jason kills women, not his expensive horses."

"Oh my God, if you hadn't been here, he would have killed me!" The reality of it hit me. "He would have killed me. What made you come here?"

"We can talk about that later," he snapped impatiently. "Is he following us?"

I looked back. "Yes. He's gaining on us. I think he wants to hit us, but he's driving crazily, swerving from side to side."

"Hang on," Adam said. We'd crested the hill and were bearing down on the bridge. He jammed on the brakes and the car fishtailed and skidded across the bridge. Adam let out a whistle of relief as my stomach did somersaults. I was so frightened I couldn't make a sound.

As we started up the opposite hill we heard the crash.

I looked back, but Adam said, "We're not stopping." Seeing my pleading look, he sighed and relented. "Okay; besides, that would make us no better than he is." He pulled into a weed-grown trail, reversed and headed back toward the bridge.

Jason's car had broken through the guardrail and plunged down the steep embankment into the stream. It lay upside down in the water, its wheels still turning slowly.

Adam was already on his phone, directing the police. "Bring an ambulance too," he added. He shut off the phone and handed it to me. "I'll pull him out before he drowns."

"Can I help?"

"No. Don't even look. I don't know what condition he's in." He scrambled down the creek bank, tangling in overgrown vines and brush and slipping on mossy rocks. In the waist-deep water he wrenched open the car door and pulled Jason out. Bracing against the current of the creek, Adam managed to drag Jason onto a sandbar. He stood beside Jason, blocking my view with his body and waited. I could hear the sirens getting closer, and then saw the flashing lights as a police car and the ambulance screeched to a stop beside me.

The paramedics half-scrambled, half-slid down to the creek and waded out to the sandbar. I saw one lift Jason's wrist and shake his head. Then they strapped him to the stretcher and brought him slowly back to the road. Following protocol, the paramedics began CPR, but soon abandoned the effort to revive him.

Blood trickled from Jason's nose and his eyes were open but no longer twinkling. My own eyes were blurred with tears, and I realized that I'd begun to shake. It dawned on me that it was all over: All the excitement, the anger, the fear, the uncertainty, the hope—all over. I'd come back to Marbury Hill thinking that I'd find a home, but instead I'd found the answer to a question I hadn't let myself ask.

I was vaguely aware of a crowd gathering and Adam answering questions. Jason was wheeled into the ambulance and it drove away, siren silenced and red light turned off. Neither was needed.

"We heard the crash and came back to see if we could help," Adam concluded, signing the statement he'd just made. He made no mention of what had gone before the crash. As far as the authorities were concerned, we just happened to be the ones first on the scene. I wondered if the pill Jason took had affected his driving, but I didn't mention it, not even to Adam.

"We'd better go tell Hattie and Nate and see if that horse is all right," Adam said, taking my arm and guiding me to his pickup. I realized we were all alone. The crowd had dispersed when the ambulance and police left, ending the reason for gawking.

When we drove through the gate, Marbury Hill looked the same: gleaming white and proud in the sunlight. "It's free now," I said, not realizing I was speaking my thoughts aloud until Adam asked, "What's free?"

"The house. It's free of the family curse."

"Are you sure?" He parked beside the garage where Jason's car had stood less than an hour before, and helped me out. I looked up at the white walls, walls Jason had had freshly painted. Was there a curse? Had it left with Jason?

"What are you going to do with it?" I asked. "You're Marian's only kin. Or do you think Jason left it to someone?"

"He couldn't. Marian was smart enough to never put his name on the deed. He didn't realize that until she was dead, and then it was too late. I'll have to do some serious thinking. I may sell it or donate it to some nature charity. Maybe I'll just give it to Hattie. God knows she's earned it." He took my hand and looked into my eyes. "Of course, with Jason gone, I may feel differently… eventually."

When Adam called Hattie into the library and told her about Jason, she didn't seem upset—or even surprised. "I knew it. As soon as I saw you, Miss Kate, I knew he was going to do something awful again." Her brown eyes shone warmly at me. "But I knew you had a fighting chance, and that you'd set things right for Miss Marian—once you got here!" she directed at Adam, swatting him lightly. She left the library, shaking her head and muttering, "took forever," but with a smile on her face.

I turned to Adam. "He really did want to kill me. And I'm sure now he pushed Marian from the window. He hung those sheets; she didn't. I should have realized it all along."

"I think he killed his first wife too," Adam said quietly.

My eyes widened. "His first wife? There was someone before Marian?"

"Joanna van Lieder. It would be almost impossible to prove, so I guess it's good that Jason's relieved us of the need to try. That's what Marian had in her special box: newspaper clippings about Joanna's death. She drowned at sea, on a luxury pleasure cruise."

I remembered what Jason had told me about how he met Marian, and felt a chill.

Adam continued, "Passengers had seen Joanna drinking heavily that night, and Marian testified at the inquest that Jason had spent the evening with her, so the death was declared an accident. I was out of the country when Joanna died and during the inquest, so I knew nothing about it. If I had, I'd have stopped Marian from marrying Jason."

"I'm not sure you could have."

He nodded. "He had a powerful appeal to women. Even you fell under his spell, and you were much more stable than Marian."

My cheeks flushed with shame over having believed Jason was a good person, or that he had any interest in me. "You were completely right about him," I admitted.

"I know. It's one of the side effects of being this brilliant," Adam said with a touch of sarcasm.

"So what made you open that box after all this time?"

"Honestly, I decided to clear you and everything that reminded me of you and of Marbury Hill out of my life. I was going to put the box in the trash, but some bit of loyalty to Marian made me open it. It seemed callous to toss away something she'd considered important." He shook his head in amazement. "Thank God I read those articles. I was horrified. Then I read her diary that described everything that happened. She saw Jason push Joanna overboard, and she let him know she'd seen him, which was stupid and dangerous. She was so infatuated with him at that point, she agreed to lie for him if he'd agree to marry her. Throughout their marriage, that perjury was the hold she had over him."

"She trusted you to know what to do with all that information." I briefly wished Marian had trusted me with it, but if Jason knew I had proof of his crime, he might have tried to kill me even before Marian.

"Did Jason know about the box?" Adam asked as if reading my mind.

"He knew she had a box, but not what was in it."

Hattie brought two cups of coffee into the library for us. We thanked her and sipped a moment in silence before setting our cups down simultaneously and looking at each other. "Kate," he said, reaching across the table to take my hands in his, "I've been kind of a jackass. I suspected Jason was up to something, but I pushed you away because I took it personally when it looked like it was working on you."

"No, I've been a bigger jackass, because it did actually work on me," I said, laughing slightly as tears threatened to well up in my eyes.

"When I finished reading, I started to call here and warn you, but I knew Jason would keep me from talking to you, and he might have even hurt you already. So I broke all the speed limits getting here."

He pulled me to my feet and put his arms around me, and I could feel the tremor that ran through him. "I came so close to losing you. What if I hadn't opened the box this morning? When you said you were coming back to Marbury Hill, I was so jealous that I almost thought you deserved whatever happened if you were foolish enough to go to Jason. But then I realized that for one thing, nobody deserves that, and for another, he'd made an actual career of doing this kind of thing. He was a professional at deceiving and hurting women, and you didn't stand a chance against that. What did he do that finally made you run?"

I told him about the cut leather strap, the yellow pills and what Nate had said about Marian's accident, shaking slightly at the memory of how close I'd come to death. "You know, I only found out about all that this morning. If I hadn't come back here, I'd never have known the truth for sure. I wonder why Jason invited me."

"I think it was the postcard you wrote him. You were right; it was perfectly cordial, but it mentioned Marian, her stories and specifically the *sea*. It all made sense after I read about Joanna's death. You said ships reminded you of what Marian had told you. He probably thought you were threatening to blackmail him."

"He counted on me to give him an alibi for Marian's murder, just like he used her to get him off the hook for Joanna's murder. God, he even used the word 'love' at one point." I shuddered at the memory.

"Did you?" Adam looked tentatively at me.

"No, even then I knew it wasn't love. I had no idea just how far from love it was, but … I realized on some level that it wasn't real." I turned to him. "But you're real. You're honest—to a fault, even—and maybe a bit reserved when it comes to showing emotion…"

"Guilty," he said smiling.

"But you're genuine. And an actual good person. And that means so much more than any superficial charm or phony drama."

"So you're saying I'm not charming…" he teased.

"Not superficially, no. But you've got your appeal," I teased back.

"That reminds me of a great joke about lawyers—" he started, but I cut him off with a kiss.

"Let's go back to Richmond and cook up some great steaks, maybe have some whiskey sours and see what happens from there," I said, referring to our chaste night at his cabin.

"I don't know," he said, frowning. "I'm not sure you have any pajamas there that would fit me."

"I'm positive I don't," I said, kissing him again.